THE McFLANNELS
SEE IT THROUGH

THE
McFLANNELS
SEE IT
THROUGH

HELEN W. PRYDE

THOMAS NELSON AND SONS LTD
LONDON EDINBURGH PARIS MELBOURNE
TORONTO AND NEW YORK

THOMAS NELSON AND SONS LTD
Parkside Works Edinburgh 9
3 Henrietta Street London WC2
312 Flinders Street Melbourne C1
91–93 Wellington Street West   Toronto 1

THOMAS NELSON AND SONS
385 Madison Avenue New York 17

SOCIÉTÉ FRANÇAISE D'EDITIONS NELSON
25 rue Henri Barbusse Paris V⁰

———

First published 1948

CONTENTS

TO
JOHN AND MARY RAMSAY

CHAPTER 1

THE PHONEY WAR

IT was a phoney war—everybody said so. There was the black-out, of course; it was a nuisance when torch batteries were what the shopkeepers called 'on short supply'; it was a nuisance, too, to have to watch that there was no chink of light showing at the edges of window blinds, for that wee fuss-pot, as Sarah called Mr. McMuslin of the flat above, was an Air Raid Warden, and nothing gave him more pleasure than to ring the door-bell when one was getting ready for bed and to insist on coming in to see what was causing the chink of light. On the whole, however, things really weren't too bad. Sarah McFlannel comforted herself daily with the thought that Matt was in essential industry and could not be called up for military service; as for Peter, he was too young to think about such things. Of course it was a phoney war! It would be over in no time!

Mr. McMuslin, though, took his ARP duties with a spurious seriousness that irritated his neighbours, a seriousness that increased with the activities of the armies in Europe. He was the kind of man who always had exact information as to the locality and extent of the latest air raid, and when the raids began to pepper northwards, he called a meeting of all the tenants of the block of flats. On being told of the function, Willie McFlannel at first protested that this was no time for parties, but was finally persuaded by his wife and family to attend. If the truth must be told, Sarah's zeal for Air Raid Precaution was rather confused with her anxiety to see inside the McMuslin flat. She went upstairs with her husband for whose preparations she had to wait so long that they were twenty minutes late, and so got an extra cordial welcome from the host and hostess, who were by this time afraid no-one at all was coming. The other tenants having judged from the opening and closing of doors that they would not be first on the scene trickled with pale patriotism to the top flat.

Mr. McMuslin constituted himself chairman, no-one else being sufficiently interested to challenge his position. He made a jerky little speech to the effect that one never knew when Glasgow's turn would come, and what were they going to do about it? One rather belligerent gentleman insisted that there was no need for all this fuss, that no bombs would ever be dropped on Glasgow; for one thing it was too far away from Germany to be worth while carrying bombs all that distance, for another there were many more important targets, and finally he had a Friend in The Air Ministry and He Knew. After that the discussion rather wandered from the point while various members of the company vied with one another in recounting the names of the friends they had in the Air Force, Mr. McMuslin being powerless to restore order until everyone was quite clear about the vast difference between having a Friend In The Air Ministry and having friends in the Air Force. The chairman, going one better, assured them that as an Air Raid Warden he had access to information direct from the Government, and while he had no desire to alarm the ladies present, he wanted to make it plain that Glasgow was next on the list of target areas, so what about making arrangements for an air-raid shelter? Shouting down the protests about the responsibility of the Town Council, he informed the meeting that there was a disused washing-house underneath the flats. He had inspected it, he told them importantly, and was convinced that if it were professionally strutted, it would be reasonably safe. When he admitted that this would involve a certain amount of expense several of the company remembered pressing engagements elsewhere. The reduced number of those present being eventually restored to attention, the matter was further complicated by a spinster lady who lived alone, and who wanted to know what protection the place would afford against poison gas. Gas, she declared, was heavier than air and would sink to the basement. Would they not therefore be safer on the top flat?

'Ach away wi' ye, missus!' said Willie McFlannel, causing

the lady addressed to wince, but whether her distress was the result of the man's rough speech or of his unfounded implication that she was a married woman, there was no means of knowing. 'If bombs was to fa' on the roof an' the buildin' caught fire, ye'd maybe no' get doon the staircase. Ah say let's get the dunny ready.'

When the more refined members of the company had had it explained what a dunny was, the business proceeded, but not for long. The ladies held matters up for a bit while they discussed which of them would sweep out and scrub the derelict washing-house. Mrs. McFlannel was finally elected to do the dirty work.

About ten o'clock Mrs. McMuslin served tea in the hope that it would stop the bickering. The bickering, however, continued accompanied by the rattle of cups and saucers and ranged over a wide variety of relevant and irrelevant topics, such as slacks for women war workers, the price of stirrup pumps, the uses to which stirrup pumps could be put, the cost of having windows cleaned and the advisability of changing the medium with which the common stairway was smeared from white pipe clay to red ditto. This last subject, in spite of all the chairman's efforts, proved the breaking-point of the increasingly strained relations between the ladies, and the party broke up in confusion. One object the meeting did achieve, however. Impressed by Mr. McMuslin's prophecies, Sarah went downstairs full of determination to put adhesive net on all the windows of their flat.

CHAPTER 2

HOME DEFENCE

SARAH chose a bright Saturday afternoon for the job of putting net on the windows to make them splinter-proof. Everybody else was out—Matt on some quiet ploy of his own, Maisie playing hockey with a team of fellow students, and Peter playing football with his school chums, while their father meandered slowly through Kelvingrove Park with the ageing Lassie at the end of a leash in conformity with the city's bye-laws. Sarah found the task more fikey than she had imagined it would be, and she was still wrestling with the second of the two kitchen windows when Willie returned from his walk. Her welcome was somewhat negative owing to the fact that she had to come down from the steps to open the door for him with a hand that seemed to have absorbed all the adhesive qualities of the net.

'Is ma tea no' ready?' grumbled Willie when he saw the chaos.

'Don't say tea to me!' snapped Sarah. 'You'll get it when I've finished this window!'

'But Ah'm that hungry ma stummuck thinks ma throat's cut!'

'Well, you'll just have to wait! I've been working at this messy job all afternoon while you were out enjoying yourself.'

In self-justification Willie pointed out that he had invited her to come with him, adding rather grudgingly, 'Will Ah make the tea?'

'No!'

'Will Ah haud the steps fur ye, then?'

'No. It's a downright shame that I should have to do it at all. It's a man's job!'

Clearly the situation called for a little tact. The man cleared his throat and said, 'Ach, Serah, but a smart wumman like you

4

is worth twa-three men. Cheer up—ye never died a winter yet !'

'Mr. McMuslin put net on all their windows,' said Sarah pointedly.

'Whit ! Thon shauchly wee n'yaff ?'

'He's nothing of the kind a shauchly wee n'yaff ! He's something big in the Corporation !'

To which Willie mumbled something about being sorry, and on being pressed for the cause of his grief he explained he was sorry for the Corporation. 'See here,' he added, 'if that shauch—if that man McMuslin can dae the job Ah'll have a shot at it mysel' if you'll get me ma tea.'

'Well . . .' Sarah considered the point. 'There's just the top pane left to do. The kettle's boiling. I'll make the tea right away.'

Willie, taking off his jacket, contemplated the task on hand. 'Ye don't mean tae tell me," he declared, 'that it took ye the hale efternune tae dab a bit net on three panes o' gless !'

'It did that ! Just you wait till you see.'

'Don't be daft ! Ah'll hae it done in five meenits—an' it'll be a bit mair evener than you've made it !' Defiantly, contemptuously, Willie strode over to the chromium-plated bird-cage which housed Joey the budgerigar. 'Hullo, Joey !' He made kissy noises. 'Nice wee Joey !—Aw, are ye no' gonnae speak tae me ?' The bird ignored his overtures and he turned accusingly on his wife. 'Here, Serah, whit've ye been daein' wi' the budgie ? He's awful peely-wally lookin' !'

'What a word to use ! Can you not *try* to speak proper ? If I was coming out for a teacher like Maisie, I'd be ashamed of my father.'

In concern, Willie remarked that he wouldn't like Maisie to be ashamed of him, but in a moment he had flared up again. 'A' the same, Serah, if you can tell me a better word fur the look on that burd's face than " peely-wally," Ah'd like tae hear it.'

The distant closing of the outside door saved Sarah the trouble of replying. 'It's Maisie,' she announced.

5

'It's a peety it's no' Matt!' retorted Willie, not without rancour. 'The tea widda been ready.'

'Are you suggesting I've got a favourite?' snapped Sarah. 'Anyway, the tea's masking and there's something in the oven all ready.'

'Jings, Ah could go a pun' o' ham an' hauf a dozen eggs.'

Sarah sneered. 'Maybe you'd like a couple of onions and a lemon thrown in to whet your appetite?'

His wife's enumeration of the articles in short supply only pained Willie, but his retort that she had no sense of humour was lost in the noise of Maisie's entrance. In a few minutes the three of them were seated round the table, father and daughter sniffing suspiciously at the contents of their plates. With masculine insistence on knowing the worst, Willie demanded, 'Whit's this?'

'It's a recipe I got from Mrs. M'Cotton,' explained Sarah.

'Well, it'll at least be cheap,' conceded Maisie as she prodded the mass with her fork.

'Ah hope it's no' like thon recipe fur soup she gied ye,' said Willie. 'Hit wis nothin' but guid watter sp'iled.'

'It's rissoles!' announced the cook with a tear in her voice.

'Ah!' exclaimed Maisie, anxious to live up to her reputation for being smart. 'Let bygones be rissoles!'

Pouring out the tea, Sarah pleaded with the other two to stop turning up their noses.

'Whit dae *you* say it is, Maisie?' asked her father.

'Well . . . I know Peter left some porridge this morning.'

'It's *not* porridge!' Sarah was indignant. Really, it was too bad! You never got any encouragement from your family to try out new things.

'I know!' shouted Maisie. 'You've been cleaning out Joey's cage!'

'That's it!' agreed her father triumphantly. 'Ah knew it! Ah seen whenever Ah came in that that burd wis huffed aboot somethin'. Nae wonder. She's pinched his seed aff 'im an' gien it tae us fur wur tea.'

'Oh, won't you taste it first?' pleaded Sarah.

6

Maisie, suddenly sorry for her mother, resolutely set herself to eat what she called 'this mess of pottage,' then, finding it good, she urged her father to taste it. A few moments later came a reluctant, 'Ay. No' bad!' from the end of the table, a remark which called forth the observation from the top of the table that that was the highest praise that had ever been known to escape the lips of a male McFlannel. The matter was still under consideration when the door-bell pealed jauntily. With a warning to her father not to pinch her portion of butter while her back was turned, the girl rose from the table and went to the door, returning a minute later to announce that Mr. McMuslin had called to discuss the arrangement of a fire-watching rota.

'Did you put him into the sitting-room?' whispered her mother.

'Yes.'

'Is't the shauchly wee n'yaff?' asked Willie, not whispering.

'Shsh,' warned his wife, but she was too late, for the gentleman himself pushed open the door of the kitchen and stepped into their midst saying:

'If you don't mind, I'll just come in here. I'm in a hurry.'

'But we're just in the middle of our tea,' protested Sarah with regrettable lack of hospitality.

'Oh, don't mind me. Don't mind me!'

'Well, will you have a cup along with us?'

'Um—no thanks. As a matter of fact, I've just had ham and eggs.' He paused for a moment to gape wonderingly at Willie who was swallowing hard after his ejaculation of 'ham and eggs,' then went on: 'As a matter of fact I just wanted to see you about a scheme I have in mind for fire-watching.'

Willie remarked that he thought all that sort of thing had been arranged by the Government, and anyway what about the dunny that Mrs. McFlannel had cleaned? But Mr. McMuslin explained that this scheme in which he was now interested was purely a private one, and did not affect any arrangement previously made about the basement. With an air of officialdom he whipped a notebook from his pocket, licked the pointed end of a pencil, and asked, 'How many of a family have you?'

7

'Oh, Mr. McMuslin!' exclaimed Sarah, 'you know quite well we've got four. Polly's married, of course, and living in Edinburgh. . . .'

'Quite-quite! But how many are actually living under your roof?'

'There are five of us altogether,' put in Maisie, who was unable to hide the amusement with which she regarded the fussy little visitor. 'But I thought the authorities already had a note of these details.'

'Oh, well, you see . . .' Mr. McMuslin made self-conscious dabs at his notebook. 'I've resigned from being a full-time warden.'

'Hoo could ye be a full-time warden if ye work in the Corporation?' demanded Willie, who was immediately silenced by his wife who asked:

'Then does that mean we don't need to worry about our black-out so much?'

'Of course it makes no difference to your black-out, Mrs. McFlannel, but we're getting away from the point. We'll take you first, miss. What's your name?'

'Marion,' said Maisie. 'Do you want my fingerprints?'

Mr. McMuslin frowned upon her. 'What night shall I put you down for duty? From dusk till dawn, you know!'

'Well, I'm working in a canteen every Tuesday night—till four in the morning.'

'Oh? Then what about Thursday?'

'That's the night I do Station Guide duty till about midnight.'

'Ah! A very patriotic young lady, if I may say so. What about Saturday then? That's giving you a night's rest in between.'

By way of being non-co-operative, Maisie said he could put her down for Sunday, and what was it all about anyway? Ignoring her question, Mr. McMuslin inquired for the names of the other members of the family.

'Matt works late three nights a week till eleven o'clock. He's got a very good position in——' Catching sight of the

8

warning look in her husband's face, she tried rather belatedly to amend it to 'in a shipyard,' but the man was too intent on his notes to pay any attention.

'What about you, Mr. McFlannel?' he asked at length. ' Can I put you down for Monday nights?'

'Naw. Ah'm on duty wi' the Home Guard every Monday.'

'What about giving up the Home Guard, then?'

'Whit!' spluttered Willie. 'Gi'e up the Home Guard! Don't be daft!'

'You may as well ask him to give up his Glasgow accent,' said Maisie.

'What about Tuesday, then?'

' He needs to get a sleep on Tuesday nights,' interposed Sarah quickly. 'He's not so young as he used to be!' Disregarding her husband's indignation at such an insult, she went on: 'And he's got parade nights Thursdays and Fridays.'

'Whit Ah want tae know is—whit's the use o' you goin' tae a' this bother when ye're no' the warden noo?' asked Willie.

'Oh, it's no bother at all, I assure you. You see I—um—it's given me a great deal of pleasure. I've got it all written down here. My idea is that there should be a contribution from each tenant towards the comfort of the team, so the first item on my list is biscuits.'

'Biscuits!' exclaimed Sarah. 'What kind?'

'Oh, any kind will do. Or perhaps you could give a carpet or a chair or a pack of cards.'

'Cuc-cards!' choked Willie. 'Whit's the cards fur?'

'Oh, bridge, of course. You see, I thought that since there were four in each team——'

' If this is a fire-watching team, you only need three,' Maisie pointed out.

'Yes, but I think it would make such a difference to have a game of bridge, don't you think. . . .'

Not sure of where all this was leading, Sarah said she had an old piece of carpet laid by, but she would like to know what it was wanted for.

'For the stair landing on the top flat, of course!'

The three McFlannels blinked at one another in bewilderment as Mr. McMuslin went on :

' I'll put you down for a carpet then, Mrs. McFlannel. You don't happen to have an old card table, do you ? No ? Well then, the next item on my list is dress. I thought it would be a good idea if we were to wear some kind of uniform—navy-blue overalls, say.'

Maisie wanted to know if he had in mind the idea of slacks for women.

' Yes, I thought it would be more serviceable, besides contributing to the general appearance, and I do think we ought to encourage everything that will foster the team spirit, don't you ! '

The McFlannels still seemed doubtful, Maisie voicing their uncertainty by asking, ' But what about a stirrup-pump ? ' Before he could answer, Sarah had nipped in with a question more to her own mind. ' What about Mrs. McMuslin ? ' she asked. ' Is *she* going to be dressing up in slacks ? '

' Well, no. You see she's making her own special contribution to the national effort, so she's exempt from this scheme.'

' Oh ? Is she making munitions ? ' asked the cynical Maisie.

' Well, no. You see she knits a great deal. She—indeed I know you'll be simply astounded when I tell you this—she can actually knit a whole sock in a fortnight ! '

' Oh, boy ! ' exclaimed Maisie. ' What does she use to cool her needles ? '

But Mr. McMuslin was off again on his scheme. ' To get back to the subject of dress, I wondered if we could perhaps wear the same colour of scarf.'

' But what about a stirrup-pump and sand and water ? ' insisted Maisie.

' Not so fast, if you please, miss. Don't you see that this list is alphabetically arranged ? I believe in having a system.'

' Ay, but mister, jist a meenit—— '

Willie's interruption was brushed aside with, ' My next item is a fire. Have you by any chance a fire of some kind, Mrs. McFlannel ? '

'But Ah thought ye were arrangin' tae pit *oot* a fire!' cried Willie, but his observation was disregarded.

'An oil stove, Mrs. McFlannel, to keep us comfortable while we're playing bridge.'

Maisie's patience was wearing thin. 'Don't you think,' she asked, 'that a better alphabetical list would have been—A for axe, B for buckets of sand and water, C for——'

Her father shouted her down with, 'But here, mister, whit aboot the bombs that'll maybe come in one o' the doonstair windaes while youse are at yer game o' bridge?'

'How can bombs come through windows!' jeered Mr. McMuslin completely ignoring all the lectures he had heard at the Wardens' Post. 'Please don't be absurd!'

'It's no' absurd!' countered Willie who, for his part, was beginning to wonder if the man had ever been a *bona fide* warden at all. 'They fa' at an angle——'

'Just a minute, Willie,' put in Sarah. 'I don't think, Mr. McMuslin, that you mentioned my name when you were making up your team. I'd be quite willing to do two nights a week to make up for the others who can't go.'

Maisie was indignant. 'Mother!' she exclaimed. 'Don't be silly! You're doing far too much already. . . .'

'Now that's very generous of you, Mrs. McFlannel, but you see I'm making the age limit for women sixty.'

'What! I'm not *near* sixty!'

'Here, mister,' said Willie, 'that's no' the wey tae talk tae a lady. See here—you've been daein' most o' the talkin', jist gi'e me a wee shot noo. A week ago Ah went along an' seen the head warden aboot this fire-watchin' business, an' he told me *they* were arrangin' official meetin's o' a' the tenants in every close, so Ah said they could have a meetin' in oor hoose— see?'

'But—but—my scheme. . . .'

'Jist you away an' pit yer scheme oot fur the paper salvage men,' suggested Willie in pity. 'Ye can tell us a' aboot yer alphabetical list at the meetin'.'

Mr. McMuslin got to his feet, the balloon of his self-importance pricked. 'Well,' he murmured, 'I won't detain you any longer.'

Sarah, still smarting under the insult to her age, could not bring herself to invite him to stay. Maisie showed him quietly to the door.

'That's his gas in a peep,' commented Willie, handing up his cup for refilling. 'Him an' 'is bridge !'

'The cheek of him !' blazed Sarah. 'Suggesting I was over sixty ! I'll never speak to him again in my life !'

'A' the same, Serah, Ah'd gi'e a lot tae see you sclimmin' up a ladder wi' troosers on. . . .'

Maisie, returning from the door, remarked that she thought the highlight of the entertainment had been the man's assertion that his wife could knit a whole sock in a fortnight. 'What d'you think she'd say, Mother, if she knew you could knit one in two days ?'

Sarah's reply was choked as she caught sight of Willie helping himself to more rissoles. In the interest of Peter who would have none for his supper, she reminded her husband of his promise to finish ' netting ' the window. 'You can't do it after black-out !' she pointed out.

'Black-out, yer granny ! Ah'll ha'e it done in five meenits !'

'Well, I'm sorry, Dad,' commented Maisie, 'that I won't be able to stay and admire you working. I've got a date.'

'When'll you be home ?' asked her mother.

'I'm not sure. I won't be too late.'

'Bring 'im hame an' Ah'll talk tae 'im,' suggested her father.

'Sorry, Dad—he only understands English.'

Leaving him to digest her jibe, she pushed the remains of a biscuit into her mouth and went off to get ready for her ' date.'

'Jings, Serah,' said Willie, 'did ye hear that nasty crack ?'

'Well, you've only got yourself to blame for the way you speak. You've been told about it often enough ! Oh, if you're going to do that job—hurry ! For goodness' sake !'

Willie rose, grumbling that he needed a moment or two in which to roll up his sleeves ; when he had taken off his collar and tie, spoken to the bird and the dog, stretched himself, fumbled with the evening paper surreptitiously, poked the fire, put on his slippers, and said, 'Ay, Ah hear ye!' several times, he laid a sudden hand on the outstretched steps in front of the window and exclaimed :

'Well, here goes! We'll shift the steps first!'

Instantly there was a gush of water thrown in his face as an earthenware basin passed on its way to the floor. Sarah screamed :

'Oh, you stupid big lump!' She screamed again. 'The bowl of water! And just look at poor wee Joey!'

'Jings! The burd's near droondet!'

'You're just the clumsiest gowk that ever was born!'

'But Ah never done nothin'!' protested Willie as he mopped his face.

'You did so! You just breenged at the steps and the bowl of water fell off.'

'Whit bowl o' watter?'

'The one I was using for wetting the window to stick the net on.'

'But whaur wis it?'

'On the top of the steps!' Sarah's tones were deliberate with mock patience as she paused in her task of wiping up the pool of water on the floor.

'Well, of a' the daft-like places tae keep a bowl o' watter——'

'The bowl's broken now, so you'll just have to climb up and down every time you want to wet the window.'

'Climb up an' doon ma foot! Ah'll gi'e the windae one slabber—I beg your pardon—I'll gi'e it one smear!'

'Well, whatever you do, get on with it and try not to be so handless. Just look at Joey's cage—all bashed in, and the poor wee bird scared to death. I don't know how I'm going to get him dry.'

'Pit 'im in the oven!' suggested Willie heartlessly. 'Here —whit side is this net gummed on?'

'Both sides.'

'Wid it no' be better tae slunge the hale piece in a pail o' watter?'

'The man in the shop said I was to wet the window first and press on the net.'

'All right, all right. Keep yer hair on.' For a moment or two there was silence while Willie contemplated his task from various angles; after that proceedings were held up while the scissors were searched for and finally unearthed in a pile of net. When the blame had finally been placed on Willie for throwing the scissors unintentionally on to the polished table and scratching it, the work proceeded, Willie seizing the wet rag his wife washed the dishes with.

'Wull Ah wet the windae wi' this cloot?'

'Yes.' Sarah turned her back as Willie climbed the steps; she couldn't bear to see the stream of water that dripped from the wet rag. Willie, for his part, was once again on good terms with himself; he smeared the window rhythmically to the tune of a song about a lovely war, 'What do we want with eggs and ham when we've got plum and apple jam. . . .' Sarah bore it stoically even when the reference to 'Form fours! Right turn!' was accompanied by vigorous dabs on the glass, but when, satisfied that the pane was sufficiently wet—a circumstance which coincided with the end of his song—Willie suggested pitching the cloth into the sink, she felt the time had come to protest.

'No!' she called, 'you'll break something!'

'Naw, Ah'll no'. Jist you watch me labbin' this cloot right intae the jawbox!'

It arrived at its destination intact, much to the 'labber's' pleasure. 'Whaur's that bit net, noo?' he demanded from his perch. Obediently Sarah fetched the article and stood back to enjoy the spectacle of him dealing with the sticky material with his wet hands. She was glad to note that he made no better job of it than she had done, and, determining to leave him in his fankle, she left the room. Willie's difficulties, however, were not borne in silence for lack of an audience, for his complaints trickled through to her in the sitting-room.

'Here, this is awful fushionless stuff. It'll no' haud ontae the windae.' Thump. Thump. 'Ech—ach—och—it'll no' stick! Are ye sure it's gummed on baith sides, Serah? Heh,

14

Serah, whaur are ye ? Are ye sure this stuff is gummed on baith sides ? It's stickin' tae ma hauns.'

She left him to his own devices, but about five minutes later she went back to the kitchen to see the result.

' It's stickin' at last ! ' he announced triumphantly.

' It's all to one side, though ! '

' Ach, well, supposin'. You're faur too pernicketty.'

' But don't you see you haven't covered the whole pane ? Come down and let me do it ! '

' Ach you ! Here, ma hauns is stuck again ! ' He writhed and wrestled while she, from the foot of the steps, pleaded with him to be careful. ' Ach ! ' he yelled, ' ma hauns is stuck tae the windae noo ! '

In spite of his wife's pleadings and warnings the man tugged in rising irritation until he upset the steps and fell, the net still clinging to his hands, to the floor, where he lay in silence. Sarah, starting out on a lecture that had as its theme ' I told you so,' stopped suddenly.

' Willie ! ' she jerked out in alarm. ' Willie ! Are you hurt ? '

Willie continued to lie in silence.

' Willie ! Speak to me ! ' She stooped down and clawed at the offensive net as though it were the cause of his silence. ' Willie ! What's wrong ? Are you hurt ? ' Then, all the exasperation gone from her voice, she got right down on her knees and whimpered tenderly, ' Willie ! Willie darling ! Speak to me ! '

The man opened one eye, a surprisingly bright eye. ' Whit wis that ye said ? ' he queried.

' Are you all right, Willie ? '

' Ah'm fine. But whit wis that ye said ? '

Catching the glint of amusement in the exposed eye Sarah's exasperation returned.

' I said—I said—you were a plowterin' footerin' gomeril ! Get up from there this very minute ! '

As was to be expected, she finished the job herself.

Chapter 3

HOME GUARD

IT was Monday evening, a week or two later. Tea was over ; Sarah, in the scullery, was washing the dishes while Maisie, in the first flush of her newly acquired teaching post, was correcting exercises at the table. Matt had drifted out as usual without specifying his destination, leaving his father in undisputed possession of the evening paper. Peter, having inherited his brother's now defunct enthusiasm for examining the works of the wireless set, was spreading himself and his hobby over half the kitchen when his mother halted him with the reminder that he had an exam hanging over his head.

' Ugh ! ' said Peter, putting the equipment back in what he hoped was its original order. ' The exam's not worrying me ! I'll get through it with both hands tied behind my back.'

Sarah gave herself a mental shrug. It was quite true. Peter had never had any difficulty with his exams. Not like Matt. Now where would Matt be bound for to-night ? Why was he so secretive ? No, secretive wasn't the word—he was quite frank when you asked him—but he always seemed to be living in a world of his own, always scribbling away on odd bits of paper. Surely, now that there was a war on, he would forget his foolish ideas about being an author. Really, you couldn't help being sorry for him when his wee stories and things kept coming back to him with those printed notices from the editors. Not that Matt looked for pity—in fact, it was just the opposite, he scowled when you said anything about editors being callous. From the thought of editors Sarah's mind passed to the kindred topic of newspapers, and from that it was just a step to the contemplation of the newspaper at her own fireside and the man behind it.

' Willie ! ' she exclaimed, ' d'you not think it's about time you were getting ready for the Home Guard ? '

'Whit's the hurry?' asked Willie. 'Are ye wantin' rid o' me?'

Sarah ignored the second question. 'I hate to see you always going off in such a rush.'

'Ach, Ah'm fine!' The newspaper was turned almost defiantly.

'I say, Dad,' said Maisie, 'I discovered to-day that one of the teachers in the school knew you in the last war. His name's McPlush.'

'McPlush!' repeated Willie in delight. 'Wee Sandy McPlush? My, Ah'd like fine tae see 'im again. Manys a time we slep' in the same flea-bag.'

'He's no chicken,' remarked Maisie.

Sarah, from the scullery, called, 'Now, Maisie, don't give your father an excuse for loitering! Willie! Look at the time.'

'Ach, lea'e me alane!'

'But you'll be late—as usual!'

'Naw, Ah'll no. Jist let me feenish ma paper.'

'You've to shave, you know!'

Willie felt his chin. 'So Ah have! Ach, Ah've bags o' time.' Once more the paper rustled with that air of defiance.

'He's still got to read the Fat Stock Prices, Mother,' commented Peter.

'It's the Stocks and Shares page he's at, Peter,' said Maisie. 'Hurry up, Dad. I want to do the crossword.'

'Ah thocht ye were correctin' exercises.'

'That's what made me think of cross words!' retorted Maisie.

'Very feeble!' said Peter with a supercilious air.

'It's as good as the pun you made at the tea-table!' Maisie seemed to feel rather insulted.

'If you two are gonnae start argy-bargyin',' said their father, getting to his feet, 'Ah may's well clear oot.'

'Thank goodness something's made you move!' sighed Sarah to herself in relief, but Willie got the echo of the sigh and demanded to know if she had made up his 'piece.'

'It's lying there in front of your nose,' said Sarah, without any clear idea of the direction in which her husband's nose was pointing.

'Did ye sew on thae buttons on ma khaki troosers?'

'I did! I sewed on three and tightened two. Really, those metal buttons——'

'Ah hope ye used steel wire.'

'I went into town specially to get the strongest linen thread!'

'Guid auld Serah. Ye're a nice wee sowl. It's a peety ye drink.'

'Willie!' exclaimed the nice wee sowl. 'Some day somebody'll believe you if they hear you saying that to me. I do wish you'd stop it!'

'Ach, cheer up. Ye never died a winter yet.' Willie rummaged around in the scullery for a bit, then shouted, 'Here, Peter, wis you usin' this razor?'

'Probably,' was the retort from the fireside, 'since it happens to be mine.'

'Well, ye micht clean it afore ye put it away!'

'I did clean it!' stormed Peter, with all the righteous indignation of a youth to whom shaving is still a novelty. 'You must have used it after me!'

'Ach, don't bother me!' barked Willie. 'Ah'm in a hurry!'

'But you're not going to use my razor just because your own is mucky!' barked Peter in reply.

'Aw, greet, bubbly! Here, Serah—you clean ma razor fur me while Ah'm away pittin' on ma uniform.'

With an air of resignation Sarah accepted the task. 'Hurry, then!' she warned him. 'You've got less than a quarter of an hour, and you know what a palaver you always have at the last minute.'

Willie made for the door, boasting, 'Ah can be oot in five meenits if Ah like!'

'Yes, if we all help you!' flung his daughter after him, but he had banged the door, missing the jibe.

Silence reigned for a moment or two till Maisie broke it to ask for help with the crossword, help that Peter failed to give as he was absorbed in a book. Seeing his absorption, Sarah advised him to put the book down as his father intended taking it with him to read during his off-duty spells, but Peter, with a snort, went on reading.

Eventually Willie returned to the kitchen, his legs surrounded by a pair of khaki trousers, the sturdiness of which appeared to make braces unnecessary ; nevertheless he yelled, ' Here, has onybody seen ma spare galluses ? Are you wearin' them, Peter ? '

' No,' replied Peter without raising his eyes. ' Are you, Maisie ? '

With rising impatience Willie appealed to his wife, ' Serah —away an' see if ye can find ma spare galluses.'

' Oh, all right. There's your shaving water ready. For goodness' sake don't make a mess in the bathroom.'

' Ah'll no' bother goin' intae the bathroom—Ah'll jist shave at the sink.' En route for the scullery he noticed Peter's pre-occupation. ' Heh, you ! Pit doon that book ! '

' Okay. Just a minute. . . . '

Once again there was silence while Willie softened his beard rather perfunctorily ; in a minute, however, Sarah was back with the information that his braces were in their usual place and why must he always leave a bedroom like a pigsty, to which Willie retorted that he didn't want to be bothered and him in a hurry.

While he shaved, Sarah took the line of least resistance and piled the table with an assortment of garments and other articles of khaki colour. ' Look, Willie ! ' she said. ' That's everything laid out for you—your coat, your jumper, your—— '

' Ma jumper ! ' repeated Willie in derision. ' Ma tunic, ye mean ! '

' Well, tunic, then. Why have you got your medal ribbons on it and not on your coat as well ? '

Willie cast his gaze heavenwards, saying, ' Allow the weemin fur askin' daft questions ! '

' Dad,' said Maisie, ' what did you get your medal for ? '

' Ah cannae mind.'

' For eating bully beef, wasn't it, Dad ! ' put in Peter.

' Naw, it came up wi' the rations. . . . Here, Peter—the

19

buttons o' ma greatcoat is awful durty-lookin'. Whit aboot giein' them a rub-up, son ? Ye're no' daein' onythin'.'

'Sorry, Dad. I've got a date with a textbook.'

'Maisie, then ?' The tone was wheedling.

'How can I ?' The wheedling tone had been used too often before under similar circumstances for it to have any influence over Maisie. 'I've got all this pile of correction to do.' She indicated the exercise books with one hand, sweeping the cross-word puzzle on to her lap with the other.

'Serah, then ? . . .'

'I've got to clear up the mess you've left in Matt's bedroom.'

'Ach, tae hang ! There Ah've went an' cut masel'. . . . . Aw, Peter son, be a sport.'

'Can I have your Wild West book, then ?'

'Okay, okay. Ehm, Maisie—that cap badge wouldnae take ye a meenit.'

'You should have done it yourself, Dad—last night.'

Sarah picked up the cap in question. 'I wish you didn't need to wear this awful-looking thing, Willie,' she said. 'With your bald head you look fair silly in it.'

'Well, whit wid ye like me tae wear ? A lum hat ?'

'I see some soldiers wearing a thing like a tammy.'

'A balmoral ? Ay, but ye've got tae be an officer in oor lot tae wear yin o' thur in the Home Guard.'

Which remark reminded Sarah of an old grievance : 'Well I'm sure you're just as able to be an officer as Mr. M'Cotton.'

'Ach, Ah cannae be bothered talkin' pan-loaf !'

'I don't believe Dad could speak English if his life depended on it !' exclaimed Maisie.

'Aw, could Ah no' ?' Willie abandoned his razor without cleaning it and advanced into the kitchen, saying, 'This is the BBC Howm Sahvice. H'yah is the Noos end this is William McFlehnnel reading it.'

'You should've said, " H'yah is the Noose and this is William McFlannel putting his neck into it," Dad,' said Peter.

'Oh, will you two leave him alone !' pleaded Sarah. 'Willie ! Look at the time !'

'Ay, Ah know.' Willie retired once more to the sink in the scullery and turned on the tap, shouting, 'Here, Serah, you button on ma galluses fur me at the back while Ah'm washin' ma face.' With a sigh Sarah fetched the braces and got to work. 'Heheheh, watch!' spluttered Willie, his face in a handful of water. 'Ye're kittlin' me!'

A few moments later, the braces dangling from his back, he emerged from the scullery pawing the air and shouting for a towel.

'Clean his teeth for him too, Mother,' suggested Peter as the towel was put into the groping hands.

Willie mopped his face. 'Aw, Maisie,' he wheedled once more, 'are ye no' gonnae gi'e ma cap badge a rub-up?'

'No, let Peter do it. He's getting something for his pains.' Reaching over, she seized the Wild West book while Peter was occupied with the greatcoat buttons, a struggle ensuing which lasted until a yell from their father stopped them.

'Serah!' he was saying. 'Ye don't mean tae tell me ye've been mairrit twenty-eight years an' ye don't know hoo tae button on galluses!' In his rage he tugged at the braces so effectively that one of the trouser buttons flew off. 'Ach, see's a safety-peen!' he roared.

'Safety-pin!' repeated Sarah. 'I'll do nothing of the kind. I wouldn't have it said that my husband went out all tied up with safety-pins. Wait till I get my needle and thread!'

'Needle an' thread yer granny! Ah've nae time fur luxuries. Get oota ma road. Whaur's ma boots? Thank goodness Ah cleaned theym last night.'

Maisie, having yielded up the Wild West book, surveyed the boots with a critical eye. 'Mphm. Your boots are fairly going to give your coat buttons a showing-up, Dad.'

Willie, too, eyed his footgear with satisfaction. 'Ay—thae's the best-polished boots in the platoon!'

'*Spit*-toon, you mean, Dad. At least that's what it sounds like when you're cleaning them.'

Willie spared a moment to send a gleam of appreciation in his daughter's direction. He would have to remember that to tell to the other chaps at the Post. He stooped to put on his boots with the remark that he didn't think his daughter would have known what a spittoon was.

'Oh, one lives and learns,' conceded Maisie.

'Now, Maisie !' urged her mother, 'don't encourage him. He's late enough as it is !'

'Does the Home Guard stamp its time on a clock, Dad ?' asked Peter, with a certain lack of respect which Sarah felt required reproof.

'Don't be cheeky to your father !' she snapped.

'Yes,' said Maisie, 'you must remember he's an old man !'

'Ah'll auld-man ye !' retorted Willie tugging at his boot-laces. 'If Ah'm an auld man, ye must be gettin' on yersel'. Ach ! Tae bleezes ! Ma lace is broke !'

'Oh dear-dear !' said Sarah. 'Tie a knot in it.'

'There's three knots in it a'readies, but !' He wrenched the mutilated article out for exhibition. 'See's anither yin !'

'Where'll I get it ?' demanded his wife.

'Hoo should Ah know ?'

Maisie suggested she should try the tool box, while Peter's notion was that the coal bunker would be as likely a place in which to find it, all of which called forth an enraged 'Shut up !' from their father.

'I don't believe there's such a thing in the house as a boot-lace !' said Sarah.

'Oh Jeengs ! You that prides yersel' on bein' sichna guid hoosekeeper ! See's a bit string, then.'

'Oh, Dad !' Maisie's tones carried pained surprise. 'Not string—surely ! What *would* the officers think !'

'You haud yer tongue !'

Peter held out a submissive hand. 'Let me see if I can tie another knot in the lace.'

'Okay. But fur the luva mike *hurry*. Maisie—see if ma gas mask's in ma haversack.'

The search for the gas mask which was not in the haversack lasted till Peter had succeeded in tying a fourth knot in the boot-lace. He handed it over, with the query, 'You wouldn't like me to pare your corns for you too, would you, Dad ?'

Maisie's comment that they must be awfully proud of Dad in the Home Guard called forth a rebuke from her mother. 'Maisie! Don't talk like that to your father! . . . See, Willie, I'm putting your piece in your haversack. Will that be all right?'

'Naw. Pit ma piece in ma pack. Or wait—Ah'll dae it masel'. Oh here, ye'll need tae get me a clean bottle fur ma milk. Ah forgot tae pit it oot when Ah came hame last Tuesday mornin'.'

'I'll just have to clean it now then, for there's not another bottle in the house that will do.'

'But Ah cannae wait till you wash oot the bottle! Here, Peter, help me on wi' ma gaiters. You dae one an' Ah'll dae the ither. Noo which is which—they're the daftest-like things Ah ever seen in a' ma born days. Ah can never mind which is top an' which is bottom.' Tossing one of the articles to Peter, he stooped to test out the other one on each ankle in turn. Suddenly he yelped. 'Ach tae hang! There's anither button away wi't. Serah, get me a safety-peen or a nail or somethin'!'

Realizing that needle and thread were now out of the question, Sarah went off to fetch a safety-pin, with the remark that she was grateful to the Powers That Be for not calling her husband out on duty every night in the week.

'Cheer up, Dad,' said Peter from the region of his father's left ankle.

'Whit noo?'

'You don't need to waste any time doing your hair.'

'Ach you! Lea'e me alane. When you're as auld as me Ah hope ye'll hae as much hair on yer heid.' For a moment or two they exchanged gaiters, each of them deciding that the one in his possession was not intended for the adornment of the particular ankle in which he was interested. Willie's irritation kept mounting; it rose higher still when Peter asked him if he had ever heard about the Home Guardsman who was so wee that his gaiters scuffed the backs of his knees. 'Ah fell oot ma cradle laughin' at that yin!' he retorted. The gaiter-exchange system worked for a few more minutes, until there was the sound of a sudden crack from the scullery and Sarah emerged.

'Oh dear-dear!' she wailed. 'That's your milk bottle broken. I was trying to scald it with boiling water. You'll just have to do without milk to-night. It's your own fault!'

Willie was furious. 'Can ye no' gi'e me a tin o' condemned milk?'

'No.'

'Ach, this is a terrible hoose. Never onythin' in it! Nae boot-laces. Nae milk bottles. Nae condemned milk!'

'There's something else we're short of too, Dad,' observed Maisie.

'Whit!'

'Time!'

'Ach, shut up, you!' Once again Willie stooped over his right ankle.

Anxious to make amends for an accident for which she was not entirely to blame, Sarah offered to put his piece in his pack to save time. This Willie refused to allow her to do. 'Ah like tae pit things in ma ain pack masel',' he insisted, a statement that started an argument between him and Peter as to the ownership of the pack in question, and Sarah had to soothe them and bring the dispute to an end by pointing out the shortness of time.

'Could you not take a wee attaché case?' she added.

'A wee attaché case!' spluttered Willie. 'Tae the Home Guard! Don't be daft! Ah'd raither hurl a pram wi' ma things in it! Heh, Peter, see's that gaiter—Ah'll pit them on when Ah get tae the post. Noo whaur's ma tunic? Maisie— see's me ower ma tunic!'

Maisie held out the tunic and, in the tones of a teacher speaking to her youngest pupil, said, 'I'll help you on with it. Will you manage to fasten it yourself, dear?'

'Aw, forget ye're a teacher!' said Willie, buttoning up the garment with fingers that fluttered with haste. When the last eye had been hooked at the neck, Peter held up a woollen pullover.

'What about this,' he asked. 'Is it worn over or under the tunic?'

Willie gaped at it in anger. 'Blast it! Well, Ah'm no' takin' aff ma tunic again. Bung it in ma—ehm—in *your* pack. Och, tae hang—thae buttons at the back o' ma tunic. Fasten them fur me, Serah. Quick!'

Sarah fumbled at the buttons, tickling him unintentionally, while Peter and Maisie stood around with his greatcoat and scarf and what Maisie called his pixie hood. There was a great deal of toe-tramping and hard breathing and recrimination before he was finally eased into his coat and belt, the proceedings being constantly held up in obedience to Willie's instructions not to hash him. He surveyed the pile of equipment on the table.

'Ah can never mind whit goes on first,' he complained. 'Should it be ma gas mask? Or ma haversack? Or ma gas cape?'

'I've got your gun here,' said Sarah soothingly.

'Ma gun!' His tones, though hurried, carried great contempt. 'Ye mean ma rifle! Noo staun' back everybody. Don't hash me. See's ma haversack.'

Peter helped him as required, although not able to assist him in the decision as to whether the water-bottle should precede or follow the gas cape in the succession of equipment that must be draped around his person. When everything seemed shipshape, Maisie rather spoiled things by producing his bayonet.

'Oh, your sword!' cried Sarah. 'Where does it go?'

'Ma sus-sword!' hissed Willie. 'Ye mean ma bayonet. Blast it—it shoulda went on first! Ease up ma haversack, Peter. Noo don't hash me!'

'Are you sure you don't need to take the mangle as well, Dad?' asked Maisie sweetly.

'Shshs!' commanded her mother.

'Wait a meenit, Peter!' Willie's voice, like his hands, shook with urgency. 'Ah cannae fasten the belt till Ah've got on the water-bottle. Shake it an' see if there's ony water in it.'

Peter shook it. Yes, last week's water (or was it that of the week before?) was still in it.

'Hurry! Hurry! Get me ma gloves, somebody!'

'Here you are!' Sarah pushed the woollen mittens into his hand. 'Is that everything now?'

' You're okay, Dad ! ' said Peter comfortingly, slapping the guardsman on the part of his equipment that was nearest his back, and added, ' Bring in the hen's meat. Here's the HLI ! '

Willie ignored the pleasantry. He seized his wife's arm. ' Come on, lass. Gi'es a wee cheeper.'

Sarah, having old-fashioned notions about propriety, resented this perfunctory duty which Willie insisted on performing no matter how great his haste, but she was too anxious to see him out of the house as quickly as possible to refuse. She held up her mouth, pushing him away at the same time.

' Be guid till Ah come back ! ' he ordered. ' So long.'

' So long, Dad. See you in the morning ! ' Peter and Maisie stood well out of his way as he rushed for the door. After it had banged on his speeding and bulky equipment the three of them collapsed into chairs, Sarah gasping :

' Oh, I feel as if I'd been out in a storm ! ' She watched her son pick up the Wild West book. ' I wonder if all the men in the Home Guard carry on like that ? '

' Impossible, Mother,' said Maisie. ' All the same, that man McPlush was telling me to-day Dad's terribly popular in the Home Guard. He said—how did he put it now ? He said if ever he was in a tight corner he'd want nobody but Dad with him.'

Sarah beamed at her daughter : ' Fancy that now ! '

Peter, with youthful contempt for the qualities of anyone over the age of twenty-five, growled, ' Well, for goodness' sake don't tell him that ! '

' Not on your life ! ' replied Maisie, who shared her brother's estimate of elderly people, although, to do her justice, she would have granted an extension in the age limit up to thirty.

The three of them sat in silence for a few minutes. Suddenly the door-bell pealed furiously. With a feeling of foreboding Sarah rushed to the door and opened it. Like a streak Willie breenged past her, gasping :

' Ah've—come—back ! Ah—forgot—ma piece.'

CHAPTER 4

'DEAR MATT . . .'

THE months went by stolidly, uneventfully as far as Glasgow was concerned. Air raids a-plenty were taking place farther south, but, except for a few false alarms when the McFlannels joined their neighbours in the make-shift air-raid shelter in the basement, there was not much change in the tenor of their ways. Then, one day Matt arrived home in the afternoon and blurted out self-consciously that he had joined the Merchant Navy. Sarah was numb with shock. She looked at the young fellow standing there awkwardly jingling the coins in his pocket.

'But, Matt,' she protested, finding speech at length. 'There was no need for you to join up!'

'I know, Mother.'

'I'm sure you're doing just as important work in the ship-yard!' There was no answer; the coins jingle-jangled irri-tatingly; why couldn't he speak up? 'Oh dear-dear!' she wailed. 'I never thought it would come to this. What made you choose the Merchant Navy anyway?'

'I—well—it seemed—sort of—adventurous.'

'Adventurous! Oh, Matt!' Sarah gaped at her son and then put her head on her arms on the table, sobbing unre-strainedly. What had come over the boy? He had never wanted adventure before. How wicked of him to do this to her! Had he not grieved her enough already by refusing to fall in with the grand schemes she had had for him as a school teacher? Suddenly the truth dried her eyes, the truth being that Matt, stupid, tongue-tied, queer though he be, had never really grieved her. Disappointed, yes! But never hurt. There he was now, dumbly trying to comfort her by patting her on the back of the neck. She reached up a hand and gripped his.

'I'm sorry, Mother,' he was saying, 'but you know I hate the shipyard. I'm just a square peg in a round hole.'

For a moment or two silence reigned between them, and they were spiritually closer than they had ever been before. Still keeping her head averted Sarah said :

' Oh, Matt, I can't bear to think of you going away and leaving me. And to the Navy, too ! Somehow the Army seems —well, safer.'

' Don't you worry about me, Mother. You're always sure of a bed of some kind in the Navy. In the Army you've sometimes got to sleep on the ground, you know.'

The woman smiled feebly, aware that he was trying to cheer her up in his own fashion. She shut her eyes firmly on the mental vision of submarines and floating mines and thirsty men clinging to rafts such as she had seen in the pictures. She longed for Willie, with whom she could share this calamity, but he was out at his work. But was it a calamity after all ? Was it not something to be proud of ? Would Dick M'Cotton show as much spunk ? All at once Matt's mother was proud of him— for the first time in his life.

During the first few weeks after Matt left home for training there was an emptiness about his room that Sarah felt every time she dusted it, but by-and-by that sensation passed off as a new pattern of life was woven round the widening interests of Red Cross work parties, canteen duties, ARP lectures ; soon she had to admit to herself, if to no-one else, that Matt was chiefly some-one to worry over—first and foremost there was his safety to worry about, and secondly there was the worry of writing letters to him. Matt, it appeared, had a knack of being much more vivid in the letters he wrote than he had ever been while at home. Long letters they were, and amusing too ! Really, he did make you laugh sometimes ! Maybe, after all, there had been some-thing in yon notion he used to have about being an author. Anyway the war would soon knock that out of him. But those long letters made it a worry to know how to answer them. There never seemed very much to say. Sarah, not having the pen of a ready writer herself, shrank from the task with increasing reluct-ance. One evening she tried to foist the duty on to her husband, making the excuse that she had a washing to do.

'Whit! Washin'!' blurted out Willie. 'Have ye no' the hale day fur tae wash in? Ah'm tired enough efter ma day's work withoot havin' tae sit an' watch you hashin' aboot!'

'So foremen *do* work!' observed Peter with some sarcasm. Like his brother before him, Peter was a disappointment to his mother, for he refused to consider 'coming-out-for-a-teacher' and had gone to serve his apprenticeship as an engineer. His interest in radio, however, took him to evening classes in the Technical College, and Sarah consoled herself with the hope that even yet he might be able to write B.Sc. after his name. It was a hope that Peter himself did nothing to foster, and she scowled at him now as he lounged over the table with the evening paper. With Maisie's help the tea-dishes were carried to the scullery while Willie continued grumbling about the prospect of a washing being done in his presence, wanting to know why it had to be done at this time of night.

'I've told you already!' said Sarah with mock patience. 'I got an emergency call-out from the WVS to-day, and I'd to stop in the middle of my washing.'

'Well, Ah'm goin' oot!' declared Willie. 'If there's one thing scunners me, it's a washin'!'

'It scunners me, too, but I've got to do it. Anyway, you can't go out! You've to write to Matt.'

'Ah never said Ah would write!'

'You should be ashamed of yourself, so you should. It's nearly three months since you wrote Matt—you that's always boasting about your son in the Navy!'

'Ach, Matt kens fine Ah'm no' a writer. Here, Peter, whit aboot you? You're no' daein' onythin'.'

'Sorry, Dad, but this is the night I do my crochet.'

'Before you start, then,' said Maisie, 'will you give me a hand to bring the sewing-machine nearer the light?'

Together the brother and sister were edging the machine nearer the lamp when their mother warned them not to bring it too near as she would be using the pulleys.

'Pulleys!' groaned Willie. 'Ach, whit kinna hoose is this?'

Ignoring his rhetorical question, Sarah produced notepaper,

a pen, and a bottle of ink, saying, 'There you are ! Now get on with it.'

Willie stared at the implements of torture. 'But whit am Ah tae say tae 'im ? ' he demanded.

'Just write the way you would speak,' suggested Sarah.

'Heaven forbid ! ' The pious plea came from Maisie, who kept on inching the machine towards the light.

'Watch where you're going with that machine,' warned her mother. 'You'll be in your father's light when he's writing.'

'Aw, don't mind me. Ah'm jist a ludger here ! ' Suddenly an idea struck the man ; he put it into words. 'Ah tell ye whit, Maisie. If you'll write tae Matt, Ah'll dae yer machinin' fur ye.'

Maisie's retort was lost in the shout that came from Sarah, wanting to know why Peter was leaving the kitchen so sleekit-like.

'I'm going to the sitting-room to do a wee job.'

'What wee job ? '

'Oh, just a wee job.'

Normally the evasiveness of the reply would have aroused his mother's suspicions, but at the moment she had two major problems to deal with—the washing and the getting a letter written to Matt ; her mental equipment being limited she could cope with no more. 'Well,' she said, ' you can't use the sitting-room. There's no fire on ! '

'But I'll not be cold ! ' Peter was half-way out of the door.

'Maybe not ! ' called his mother after him, ' but you'll be using light. You can do your wee job in here.'

'No, I can't ! ' The door slammed as Sarah caught sight of her husband toying with the *Radio Times*.

'Willie ! ' she exclaimed. 'Put that down and get on with Matt's letter ! '

'Ach, but Serah, there's a wee play comin' on ! '

'I'll wee-play you ! You're some father, so you are ! '

'Ach, you ! ' Willie flung down the BBC programmes with disgust and took up the pen with more disgust. Seeing the pen actually in his hand, Sarah felt justified in going to the scullery —and her washing. Half the battle, she felt, had been won. She turned on the hot water tap.

30

'Heh, Serah, this pen'll no' work!' called Willie above the din of the running water.

'It was all right this morning when I was using it!'

'Ay, but whit wis ye usin' it fur? A screw driver?'

'Oh, don't put off time! The address goes at the top right hand corner.'

'And the date is——' began Maisie, when her father snapped:

'Ay-ay, noo don't hash me!' He sat down at the table to the intense relief of his wife, but her peace of mind was shattered in a moment when he called, 'Heh, Serah, this table's awful shoogly.'

'Well, put a book under the bad leg.'

Unfortunately at that moment Maisie began to operate the sewing-machine and the noise of it, coupled with that of the running-water tap in the scullery, somewhat blurred Willie's impression of his wife's instructions.

'Who's got a bad leg?' he wanted to know, glad of any red herring drawn across the letter-writing track.

Sarah's hearing, too, was blurred, and she called back, 'A book!'

'A dook?' Willie was bewildered. 'Who's goin' fur a dook?'

Turning off the tap and silencing Maisie's efforts, Sarah came to the table and said quietly, 'I said—put a book under the bad leg of the table to even it up.'

'Oh, Ah see! Whaur'll Ah get a book?'

'The *Radio Times* should do,' suggested Maisie.

'The very dab! Noo whaur did Ah put it? Oh, here it's!'

Unsuspectingly Sarah returned to the scullery as Maisie resumed her treadling. In a moment or two they were supplied with the gratuitous information that there was Scottish Dance Music going on at that moment according to the *Radio Times*. As if to corroborate his statement Willie switched on the wireless set, and the sound of piobaireachd was added to that of running water and the sewing-machine. 'Boys-a-boys!' he exclaimed, 'that's the stuff tae give the troops!'

'Willie!' Sarah stormed back into the kitchen. 'Put off that wireless set and get on with your letter!'

'Ach, Serah, have ye nae music in yer blood?'

'Not that kind anyway!' she replied, switching off the set for him.

'Ach, you! Here, this *Radio Times* isnae thick enough fur evenin' up this table.'

'Double it, then,' said Maisie.

'Ah'd like tae double it oota here!' The man went down on his knees and eventually got the steadiness of the table to his satisfaction. Rising, he announced that he would just have a draw at his pipe before starting to write.

'You'll do nothing of the kind!' commanded Sarah.

'Ach, Serah, you'd never dae fur a foreman!' He picked up the pen once more and sat down, but was on his feet in a moment with the complaint that the light was not very good.

'It's okay by me, Dad,' said Maisie, 'and I'm doing finer work than you.'

'If ye ask me,' he said, ignoring the observation, 'that lamp hasnae been cleaned for a sixmonth. Ah'll jist gi'e it a wipe the noo.'

'No, you won't!' Sarah snapped. 'D'you expect the rest of us to sit around in the dark while you're cleaning the bulb, eh?'

'Ach! Talk aboot bein' henpecked!' He sat down again and spent a leisurely five minutes writing the address on the notepaper as well as some rectangles on the blotting-paper. The washing and machining motions went on noisily. Suddenly he exclaimed that he had blotted the notepaper; he tore the sheet off the pad and was about to throw it into the fire, when his wife reminded him of the necessity for saving every single scrap of paper.

'It can go in the salvage bag,' she concluded.

'Whaur dae ye keep hit?' he inquired with suspicious eagerness.

'In the lobby press,' answered Sarah, adding, as she saw him make for the door, 'no-no! Not just now! You can put it away after you're done.'

'Ach, Serah, Ah tellt ye a'readies—you'd never dae fur a

foreman.' He sat down once more and had laboriously achieved a new copy of the address on the top right-hand corner of the paper, when the door opened and Peter came in with an awkwardness no-one noticed. His father greeted him with delight. 'Hullo, Peter, come on ower here an' gi'es yer crack!' He made room for his son at the fireside.

'Willie!' The warning came once again from the region of the scullery.

'Ah wis jist wantin' 'im tae gi'e me a haun' wi' writin' this letter!' expostulated the injured man.

The look he got from his wife sent his head bending once more over his literary effort. He scraped away in silence for a moment or two; then, as though to encourage himself, he read aloud what he had written: 'Dear Matt, I hope this finds you as well as it leaves me.' As he looked round for further inspiration, his curiosity was aroused by Peter's behaviour. 'Heh—whit's that ye've got there?' he demanded.

'Oh, Willie!' Sarah's tones carried exasperation, reproof, correction; indeed an impartial listener might have jumped to the conclusion she was in a nagging mood.

'Peter's hidin' somethin' up 'is jook!' To Willie the excuse was watertight, but all Sarah thought of it was contained in her brief 'huh!' As an afterthought she added:

'You leave Peter alone. It's Matt you've got to think about.'

'Ach, you!' Once again Willie looked at what he had written. Acting on the principle that the village pump yields up water when a little water is poured into it, he read his composition aloud once more: 'Dear Matt, I hope this finds you as well as it leaves me.' He closed his eyes in an agony of concentration while the sounds of the sewing-machine, the running water, the creaky wringer all flowed past him unnoticed. He opened them with a start as a new noise was added—that of a tortured violin. 'Whit the heck wis that?' he demanded, in such astonishment that Maisie stopped the sewing-machine to gape at her brother.

'My sainted aunt!' she exclaimed. 'Peter's got a violin!'

Turning off the running water, Sarah advanced into the kitchen, saying, ' What's this now ? '

' It's too cold for my hands in the sitting-room,' explained the lad, ' so I'll just need to practise in here.'

' But whaur did ye get the fiddle ? '

' I've had it for months. I've been keeping it at the works— practising at the meal hour. I'm to play at the concert to-morrow.' Partly out of embarrassment and partly out of bravado, he drew what had once been part of a horse's tail across what had once been part of a sheep's entrails—with the appropriate effect of an animal in pain.

' Jings ! ' His father's astonishment knew no bounds. ' Oor Peter's a Works Wonder ! '

' But, Peter ! ' sniggered Maisie, ' you've got no more music in you than a wheelbarrow has.'

' That's what *you* think ! You'll have something different to say when you hear the concert broadcast.'

Peter's audience reacted according to their individual temperaments ; his father's exclamation registered unbelief, his sister's horror, while his mother's ' Oh, Peter ! ' was pure ecstatic pride. To show that his previous caterwaul had not been a flash-in-the-pan, he drew the bow across the strings once more.

' Oh, stop ! Stop ! ' screamed Maisie. ' That's awful ! '

' Never mind her, son.' Willie's tones were encouraging and not without ulterior motives. ' Ye're daein' fine ! Gi'e's a wee tune—say—" Annie Laurie." '

For once Sarah was oblivious to her husband's manœuvres. ' Oh, Peter,' she beamed, ' why did you never tell us you could play the violin ? '

' Oh,' said Peter with becoming bashfulness, ' I wanted to keep it for a surprise. I—I'm playing in the band at the concert to-morrow, and I just wanted to run over my part.'

Maisie got to her feet, saying, ' Not in my presence ! '

' Ach, sit doon, lass ! ' commanded her father. ' On ye go, Peter. Let's hear " Annie Laurie." '

But Sarah awoke to his antics. ' Willie ! ' she exclaimed. ' Are you forgetting you're writing to Matt ? Peter—away you go back to the sitting-room. If your hands are cold you can put on your gloves.'

'Oh, Mother, don't be daft ! How can anybody play the violin with gloves on ? '

'Seems a jolly good idea to me,' put in Maisie. 'Help to muffle the sound.'

'What's wrong with you,' snapped Peter, 'is that you don't know good music when you hear it. Just listen to this.' By way of illustration he tucked the instrument of torture under his chin and made several noises similar to the ones he had produced before.

'Sounds like a sick hyena,' pronounced Maisie.

'That was the *The Tales of Hoffman*,' explained the musician. 'And you can cut out any nasty cracks about the tails of cats— I've heard them all.'

'I'm afraid I didn't recognize the masterpiece.' Maisie's expression was lofty.

'Of course, I don't play what *you* would call the top line.' Peter was spoiling for an argument.

'Oh, be quiet, you two ! ' ordered Sarah. 'How can your father write a letter with that noise going on ? Away you go, Peter.'

Peter got up and went out, slamming the door behind him. Maisie resumed her machining, Sarah hung some clothes on the pulleys, while Willie surveyed his handiwork, and, as though to commit the immortal words to memory, read them aloud all over again : 'Dear Matt, I hope this finds you as well as it leaves me.' He stared at the empty space of notepaper beneath his writing. Suddenly he exclaimed, 'Heh—who's been spittin' on ma letter ? ' He looked up and glowered at his own heavy underwear that had been inadequately passed through the creaky wringer. 'Ach—this is nae place fur me ! Ah'll away ben the hoose aside Peter. Ah can feenish writin' ma letter in there.'

When the cause of his discomfort had been explained to Sarah and she had removed it without giving him permission to leave the room, Willie tore off the blistered page and started another one, with the grouse :

'If Matt knew the bother it wis tae me, he'd be the first tae say, "Don't write, Dad"! Whit date did ye say it wis, Maisie?'

While Maisie was telling him, the doorbell rang.

'Ah'll go!' announced Willie, getting to his feet with alacrity.

'No, you won't!' said Sarah, pushing him down into his chair. 'You're not usually so keen. I'll go myself. You get on with that letter.'

As she opened the kitchen door the wail of Peter's violin reached them; as soon as it was closed behind her, Willie put on a wheedling act.

'Aw, here, Maisie, whit aboot you writin' this letter fur me? Ah could copy it.'

'No fear.'

'D'ye think that'll be somebody comin' in?'

Maisie listened for a moment. 'It's the woman next door,' she said. 'Mother won't ask her in.'

'Ach, that gabbleguts! She'll be at the door fur ages. Here—Ah'll jist ha'e a couple o' draws at ma pipe. Noo whaur did she plank thae matches?'

The clock was striking nine as Sarah came back into the kitchen, saying, 'Would you look at the time! I thought that woman would never go away—standing there blethering all about her mother's operation. Here, Willie—are you never finished with that letter yet?'

'Och, we're comin' on. Ah'm jist goin' tae listen tae the News. Away you go and get on wi' yer washin' an' never mind me.'

Sarah was too worried about the time she had lost at the door to argue with him, so he listened with all his attention to the latest information about the progress of the war. After the News came a 'pep' talk and, between one thing and another, it was ten o'clock before he took up the pen again. Peter drifted in with a hungry look.

'Hullo, Dad!' he said. 'How's the letter going? Finished?'

'Ach, shut up!'

'How many pages have you written?' asked Maisie.

'Ah've written aboot an inch an' a hauf! Listen: "Dear Matt, I hope this finds you as well as it leaves me. The weather here is fine for this time of the year."'

'Oh, Dad!' exclaimed Maisie, 'I don't think you should say anything about the weather. You never know—the censor mightn't like it.'

'Well, whit the bleezes am Ah tae write aboot?'

'You could tell him we're wearying to see him,' suggested Sarah.

'And you could say that Peter fancies himself as a violinist now,' was Maisie's contribution.

'And that Maisie's going with another boy-friend,' was Peter's, delivered with a certain amount of rancour.

'Fur peety's sake,' cried Willie frantically, 'will yez lea'e me alane! "Dear Matt, I hope this finds you as well as it leaves me. Dear Matt, I hope this finds——"'

'You could tell him we're expecting Polly and wee Ian to stay with us next week,' said Sarah.

'Yes, and that the woman next door's mother has had an operation,' put in Maisie.

'And what about telling him that Mother——'

Peter's bright idea was drowned in the yell that came from the scribe at the table: 'Will yez a' shut up!'

'Willie!' warned his wife, 'there's no need for you to lose your temper. We're only trying to help you. Tell Matt that fish is awful scarce just now and that it's a terrible price.'

'Whit's that got tae dae wi' Matt?' stormed Willie. 'D'ye think because he's in the Merchant Navy——'

'Oh, stop arguing!' Sarah flung over her shoulder as she went back to the scullery and her washing.

'You could tell him thon piece of news I gave you about Queen's Park,' said Peter.

'Whit wis that?'

'Ugh, you remember, Dad! I read it out to you from the paper at tea-time.' Peter reached for the newspaper and began to read: '"The Queen's Park Football Team——"'

Willie interrupted him with a snort. 'Queen's Park! That's

37

no' a team—it's a dancin' class! Ah tell ye, the Rangers could——'

It was Peter's turn to snort. 'The Rangers! I've spent a better afternoon with the toothache——'

'But Ah'm tellin' ye——'

'Willie!' Sarah shouted above the torrent of water in the sink. 'Be quiet! Get on with your letter!'

'But hoo can Ah get on wi' ma letter when he's tryin' tae ram doon ma throat that Queen's Park is a fitba' team?'

'Peter,' said Sarah, 'you should have more sense than to start an argument just now!' Turning to her husband, she adopted a wheedling tone, 'Come on, Willie——'

'Ach, tae hang wi' this letter. Ah'll feenish it the morn's nicht.'

'You'll finish it this night, supposing you don't get to bed till it's time to get up!'

'Is't no' near supper time? Ma stummuck's rumblin'.'

'I can't set the supper till you're done with the table,' said Sarah as she turned back to the scullery.

' "Dear Matt," ' groaned Willie, ' "I hope this finds you as well as it leaves me. . . . Dear Matt, I hope this finds you as well as it . . ." '

'Mother!' demanded Peter, 'could we not have our supper off the bunker? I'm starving.'

But it was after eleven o'clock before Sarah was finished with her washing. Maisie shut up the sewing-machine as she asked, 'Come on, Dad, how many pages have you written?'

'Hunners!' replied Willie.

'What have you said?' The girl leaned over her father's shoulder as she read: ' "Dear Matt, I hope this finds you as well as it leaves me. The weather here has been fine for this time of the year." '

'We told you to leave that out, Dad!' said Peter.

'Oh, leave it!' said Sarah. 'It's always something.'

Maisie went on reading: ' "You will be surprised to hear that Peter is now a famous violinist. The BBC has asked him to broadcast——" '

'I never said any such thing,' blazed Peter. "It's not true !
I only said——'

'Oh, leave it !' was Sarah's advice. 'Maybe it'll be true by
the time Matt gets the letter. Go on, Maisie. What else has
he said ?'

'Something about me, I'm afraid. What's this ? "Maisie
is going-set with another chap. I don't know how many this
will be. There is word of him being asked up for a ham and
egg tea, so I expect it'll be serious. I don't know what Maisie
sees in him, for they tell me he's a shauchly wee n'yaff." ' Maisie
glared at her father. 'Dad ! That's an insult ! I won't have
you saying things like that about George ! I've a good mind to
tear up your old letter !'

'Oh, leave it, Maisie,' said Sarah for the third time. 'Matt
knows your father doesn't mean half he says.'

'But it's not fair ! Matt'll think I'm a poisonous wee peuk
that's got nothing in her head but boys !'

'Oh, be quiet, Maisie,' implored Sarah. 'You can write
Matt yourself and tell him the truth. Dad will have his little
joke. Let's hear the rest of the letter.'

Maisie resumed her reading, her face still flushed with annoyance : ' "Your mother is as sonsy as ever. She weighed herself
last week. Fancy—fourteen stone five pound——" '

'Willie McFlannel !' Sarah's rage knew no bounds. 'How
dare you say a thing like that ! You'll just tear up that letter
and write a new one. The very idea ! I am *not* fourteen stone !
Come on, Maisie—give me that letter till I tear it up !'

'But, Mother, you've just told us that Matt knows what
Dad is !' Peter pointed out.

'Yes,' said Maisie, 'and that he will have his little joke.'

'That's different. He's not going to write lies about
me !'

'Mother !' said Peter. 'Remember what you said about me
and the BBC ? "Maybe it'll be true by the time Matt gets the
letter." '

But that was no comfort to Sarah.

'Ach, can ye no' dae whit ye've jist tellt Maisie tae dae !'

39

queried the unfortunate letter writer. ' Can ye no' write tae 'im yersel' an' tell 'im whit weight ye are ? '

That was the wrong thing to say, as he very soon discovered. To quieten down the storm he suggested that supper should be served, only to find that that too was a tactical error. In a moment or two he was at work on a new version, and while he laboured at it the rest of the family kept silence. At length he flung down his pen with an air of triumph.

' Well, that's that done at last ! ' he announced. ' Bring on the ham an' eggs.'

' What have you said this time ? ' asked Maisie with justifiable suspicion.

' Did you say thon about me weighing fourteen stone ? ' demanded Sarah.

' Ah did nut ! '

' Well, then, it doesn't matter what else he's said, Maisie,' said Sarah. ' We'll get the supper set.'

' Just a minute ! ' Maisie began to read aloud. ' " Dear Matt, I hope this finds you as well as it leaves me. You will be sorry to hear that Peter has not been asked to play the violin by the BBC. Maisie is fine and still going with the boys. Her latest is coming up for a ham and egg tea soon, so it must be serious again. She says he is not a shauchly wee n'yaff, but we'll just have to wait and see. Your mother is as sonsy as ever——" '

' Willie ! You—— '

Maisie ignored the interruption. ' " but she won't let me tell you what weight she is. I could be doing with another pipe, so if you come across one, don't forget Your loving father, W. McFlannel." '

' Well, I suppose it could have been worse,' said Sarah with a sigh of relief. ' Come on, Maisie. Help me to set the supper.'

As she spoke the door-bell rang and they all gaped at one another. Who could it be at this time of night ?

' I bet you that's the morning's milk,' said Peter with a good deal of feeling.

' It could be the folk down the stair up to complain about Dad's pen scratching.'

'Peter, away you go and see who it is!' ordered his mother.

As the young fellow went to the door Sarah flung a table-cloth over the table, Willie protesting that he still had to write the envelope—if he could summon up enough energy after such an exhausting night's work. They could hear a commotion in the hall. Sarah, wide-eyed, clutched her jumper. Why should she suddenly feel so excited?

Peter rushed into the kitchen. 'Oy! Look who's here!' he yelled. 'Matt!'

Matt it was. His mother threw herself into his arms sobbing with delight. Maisie tugged at his coat sleeve for a little recognition. Peter slapped him heartily on the back asking where his parrot was. As for Willie, he contemplated his literary achievement.

'Help ma boab!' he ejaculated, more in frustration than welcome, 'Dear Matt!'

CHAPTER 5

WILLIE IN HOT WATER

MATT was changed; they all realized that. But how deeply or how permanently none of them had any chance of assessing, for his leave lasted only a few hours, just long enough for Matt to demonstrate that he had lost his diffidence, his 'round-O-ness,' his air of being a misfit. He was gone again before even his mother could get near to him spiritually, and in less than a week the household had settled down once again to its wartime routine.

One evening Willie, seated by the fire and ostensibly reading the evening paper, turned round as Peter came into the kitchen and snapped :

'Heh, can ye no' shut the door efter ye ? Ye'd think ye'd been born in a park !'

As Peter went to close the door Sarah peered at her husband with the remark, 'Good gracious, Willie, what's the matter with you to-night ? You've done nothing but girn since ever you came home from your work.' She paused as a bout of sneezing made Willie too preoccupied to heed her ; when he was quiet again she resumed, 'I think you've got the cold if you ask me.'

'Ah didnae ask ye !' At that moment a creaky sound reached them from the flat below. 'Here !' he bellowed sniffily. 'Did you tell that wumman doon the stair tae ile 'er pulleys ?'

'Ugh you !' Sarah's reply was evasive. 'You're a carnaptious old curmudgeon to-night.'

But Willie was in no mood for evasion. 'HAVE ye tellt 'er ?' he demanded.

'I have not ! Catch me going to anybody's door and telling them to oil their pulleys !'

Any retort that Willie might have made was lost in another fit of sneezing ; when it had passed Maisie suggested that the doctor ought to be called in.

'That's right,' put in Peter with melancholy sarcasm. 'It sounds like mortification setting in.'

In the middle of Willie's nose-blowing the sound of the un-oiled pulleys reached them again. Taking off a slipper Willie rattled the heel of it against the skirting board at the fireplace. 'There !' he barked, fending off Sarah's restraining hand. 'Ah hope the plaster's off their ceilin'.'

'You bad-tempered old heathen !' exclaimed Sarah. 'How am I going to face her in the morning after you knocking down on her like that ?'

Willie's only reply was another sneeze and a complaint that his handkerchief was 'wringing.'

'He's getting worse, Mother,' observed Peter. 'Double-barrelled sneezes now. I suggest a hot foot-bath.'

'I'm going out, then,' said Maisie. 'I don't want to be asphyxiated.'

'Something'll have to be done at any rate,' said Sarah. 'And it'll have to be me that'll do it, for I needn't expect you to do anything for yourself, Willie."

'Ach, stop greetin',' advised the sneezer, beginning to feel persecuted.

'Cheer up, Dad,' said Peter with the air of one who likes to say 'I told you so.' 'You never died a winter yet !'

'You shut up !'

Sarah got to her feet with a sigh, putting away her knitting. She had been indulging in the luxury of making a fancy jumper for herself, a relief from the interminable rough socks ; it seemed hard that her few pleasures should be so curtailed. 'I suppose it'll have to be a foot-bath,' she said. 'You can start taking off your slippers and socks while I get ready.'

'Fur the luva mike, Serah, stop palaverin'. Lea'e me alane.'

But Sarah, having had to sacrifice her own pleasure, was determined to make others suffer the same self-abnegation. 'Maisie,' she called, 'stop that crossword and get the wee bath from the lobby press. Peter, you spread some newspaper on the rug there in front of the fire.'

Maisie was not doing too well with the crossword, so her

response was more or less immediate ; Peter, however, was indignant and said so, putting great emphasis on the fact that it was the first free evening he had had for weeks owing to working late. His father cut into his complaints with a roar :

' Heh, Maisie, SHUT THAT DOOR. There's a draught like tae caw the feet f'ae ye ! '

Maisie shut the door, but not until she had returned with the utensil for which she had been sent.

' This wee bath is full of dross, Mother,' she pointed out.

' I tell you what,' said Peter. ' Make him sit up on the sink with his feet in what he calls the jawbox.'

' Splendid idea ! ' agreed Maisie. ' He could give us a running commentary on what's going on in the street.'

' Yes ! ' Peter was growing more and more enthusiastic. ' And you and I could run out every now and then and cry " coohooey " up to him.'

' Shurrup ! ' snarled Willie, stopping his nose-blowing to make the remark.

' That's enough, you two,' said Sarah. ' Peter, you get yon big zinc bath from below your bed. It's full of semmits and—things. So be careful.'

' But, Mother, it's not me that's got the cold. Let Dad do his own dirty work.'

To which Maisie appended a fervent ' hear-hear.'

' Well, it just means I'll need to go and get it myself,' sighed their mother.

' Ach,' exclaimed Willie adenoidally, ' Ah don't know whit ye're makin' a' the fuss aboot. Ah'm fine ! ' As if to put an exclamation mark to his statement, he sneezed violently and then demanded a fresh handkerchief.

' Here's a clean one of mine,' offered Maisie.

' Ah said a hankie—no' a dabbity ! '

' Oh, give him a tablecloth,' suggested Peter on his way to the parlour where his bed was. While he was still rummaging about amongst the collection of receptacles stored beneath the bed the door-bell rang.

' There you are ! ' said Sarah from the scullery. ' That'll be

Mrs. McDruggit up to complain about you knocking down on her, Willie. If it wasn't for that cold you've got, I'd make you go and face up to her yourself.'

'Tell 'er tae come in,' was the affable suggestion.

'I'll do nothing of the kind. You have your slippers and socks off by the time I come back.' And Sarah left the kitchen with such a whirl of righteous self-pity that the closing door sent a shiver of discomfort prickling up her husband's spine. He huddled nearer the fire, his fresh handkerchief to his nose. After a moment or two he said :

'Heh, Maisie, ma throat's gettin' sair. Ah hope Ah'm no' in fur somethin' serious.'

Maisie bent a teacher-like solicitude over her father. 'Let's see your tongue. Maybe it's scarlet fever or diphtheria.' At that Peter returned with the required zinc bath, and, having closed the door with his foot, he was immediately called upon by Maisie to recall whether or not she had had a running nose as a preliminary symptom of the diphtheria she had had as a child.

'Considering I was about the height of two scrubbers when you had diphtheria, I don't see how I can be expected to know,' retorted Peter.

'Come on, Dad. Shoot out your tongue.' Maisie looked critically at the reluctantly exposed organ. 'Mphm. It's pretty mucky, isn't it, Peter !'

Peter in turn took a distant view. 'Not half !' he said with gusto. 'It's like——'

His simile was strangled at birth. 'Never you mind whit it's like. See's me ower a mirror tae Ah see fur masel'.'

'Would you like us to take down the overmantel, or would a hand-mirror do ?' inquired Maisie.

'Nane o' yer lip. See's thon shavin' mirror f'ae the scullery.'

'Here's a wee one from my handbag.'

By dint of jouking this way and that, Willie at last focused his face into his line of vision in the light of the lamp. He swallowed to give himself courage. 'Ach, ma throat's gettin' waur !' he announced. Peering into the mirror, though, he failed to gain any information, on account of the fact, he contended, that it was like the Black Hole of Calcutta. 'See if *you* can see onythin', Maisie.'

'O.K. Come over to the light.'

Obediently Willie came, and in further obedience said ' Ah !'

' Boy ! What a filthy tongue ! And *what* a smell off your breath !'

' Shsh, Maisie,' warned Peter. 'Your best friends don't tell you. . . .'

Willie looked a shade paler as he asked, ' Wis *your* tongue dirty when *you* had dip'theria, Maisie ?'

At that moment Sarah opened the door, catching the last few words of her husband's query.

'What !' she exclaimed. 'Are you putting ideas into his head, Maisie ? It's nothing but a cold he's got.'

Willie's momentary fear turned to indignation. 'Nothin' but a cold !' he ejaculated. 'Ah like that ! An' me maybe dyin' on ma feet wi' dip'theria ! Here—is there no' a *Doctor's Book* in the hoose ?'

' I'll *Doctor's Book* you !' Sarah bustled to the scullery. ' You'll put your feet in hot water and then get into bed. You'll be all right in the morning.'

' Hoo dae *you* know ?'

' See !' She splashed a basinful of steaming water into the zinc bath near Willie's feet as he collapsed into his chair again in self-pity. ' It's a shame, so it is, you going and getting this cold and the M'Cottons coming to-morrow night.'

' If it's diphtheria he's got, it'll be a rare excuse for putting them off,' declared Peter with a good deal of feeling.

' Jings !' gulped Willie, now thoroughly frightened, ' Ah hope it's no' dip'theria. Ah—Ah'm feelin' awful hot-kind. Whaur's that *Doctor's Book* ?'

' Oh,' said Sarah, ' you're nothing but a wean ! See—take off your socks.'

' But if it's dip'theria, maybe it'll no' be guid fur me tae wet ma feet !'

' Oh, Dad,' said Peter in mock horror, ' surely you wouldn't disgrace the family by going into hospital with dirty feet !'

'Whit! Hospital!' Willie gaped from one to the other of his nearest and dearest. He squared his shoulders manfully 'Ah'll no' go! Ah've never been in a hospital in ma life, an' Ah'm no'——' but the rest of his resolution was lost in a fit of coughing, the blame for which Sarah placed on Peter and Maisie for tormenting him.

'Cheer up, Dad!' said Maisie, undeterred by her mother's flyting, 'we'll come to the gate every Saturday and ask for you. Whether would you prefer white roses or black grapes?'

Ignoring the thoughtful suggestion, Willie reached out a hand to his wife who was tugging at his slippers. 'Serah—ye widnae let them take yer auld man away tae a hospital?'

'Ugh, you! Come on! Off with your socks!' She got them off eventually. 'Now—in with your feet. There!'

With a splash Willie's resisting feet were plunged in the steaming bath. 'Yow!' he yelled. 'Ye're scaudin' me.'

'Don't be a baby!' Sarah tried unsuccessfully to push the tortured limbs back into the water.

'Well, you try pittin' *your* feet in there! Whit wey is the watter yella?'

'Mustard. Come on! A foot-bath's no use unless it's hot. Roll up your trousers a bit—they'll get wet.'

Rolling up his trousers obediently, Willie ordered Maisie to bring a jugful of cold water; while she was fetching it Peter observed that it was surely about time for another sneeze. Alarmed, Willie wondered what could have gone wrong that his nose seemed to have stopped running so suddenly.

'It's the cold,' said Sarah calmly. 'It's gone down to your throat.'

Willie swallowed, felt his neck, and sniffed while waiting for the cold water to arrive; when Maisie produced it, there was a tussle as to which of them should pour it into the bath, with the result that most of it was splashed on to the bare feet that were so anxious not to be scalded.

'Look whit ye've went an' done!' yelled the invalid. 'Enough tae gi'e me ma daith o' cauld. Ah'm a' shiverin' noo.'

47

'The bath should be cool enough for you now,' said Sarah. 'Come on——'

'Jist a meenit. Ah'll feel it wi' ma toe first !'

'Oh, stop swithering !' Sarah had brought up four young children ; she was determined not to be over-ruled by this elderly baby. In a moment Willie was yelling again.

'Heheheheh ! Let go ma legs ! Hohohohohoh ! That water's still bilin' ! Oh ! Oh !'

'You'd better bring another jugful of cold water, Maisie. We can add hot afterwards !'

En route for the scullery, Maisie exchanged a look of scunneration with her brother, their father meanwhile demanding once more that the *Doctor's Book* should be brought to him as his throat was getting worse.

'Oh, I suppose you'll not be happy till you get it !' said Sarah. 'Peter, away you go and look for it—in the room press.' As Peter uncoiled himself from the task of finishing Maisie's crossword, she added, 'Now, don't go and make a midden of the place looking for it.'

'I'd rather be in the midden than the nursery !' muttered Peter as he left the kitchen, but his preference passed unnoticed, as the others were absorbed in the task of pouring a jugful of water carefully into the bath that was already half full of tepid solution of mustard.

'Ah wis jist thinkin',' said Willie when his feet were out of sight, 'wid Ah no' be better tae hae ma bunnet on ? Ma heid's kinna shivery.'

'What about your lum hat, Dad ? We could light a candle inside it—that would keep your head warm.'

'Here, Maisie—if you were as no'-weel as me ye widnae be sae skeigh. Get me ma bunnet aff the ballstand.'

'Anything else ?' asked Maisie as she opened the door.

'Ay ! Shut the door !'

Left together, Sarah and Willie looked at each other, both of them in self-pity ; then a surge of remorse flowed over the woman. Reaching over to the bed, she grasped the down-quilt which she wrapped round her drooping husband.

'Oh me,' complained he, 'Ah'm sair forfaughen!' He peched loudly as the quilt was tucked round about him. 'Eh—Serah——' He broke off hesitantly.

'Yes, Willie?'

'Ye're awfu' guid tae me.'

'Ugh, that's nothing!' retorted Sarah briskly to offset the feeble foolishness of her baby-man. 'Just you hurry up and get well again. I'm going away to get you a hot drink now.'

'Never mind the drink!' Willie's hand fumbled its way out of the quilt and detained her. 'Ehm—Serah——'

'What is it?' The tone was patient, almost tender; after all, men were helpless bit things that couldn't get along without a woman to look after them—well or ill.

'Ah'm thinkin' Ah havenae been an awfu' guid man tae ye, lass.'

'Hoots, Willie—you're not to talk as if you were dying.'

'Ah—Ah'm sorry for a' the nasty things Ah've said tae ye. Dae—dae ye think ye could gi'e me a wee cheeper?'

'You're an awful man!' she said, but all the same she yielded to the pressure of the hand that held her arm and bent down her mouth to the germ-laden one of her man. To cover her embarrassment, she tucked the quilt around him quite unnecessarily.

'D'ye know if ma insurance policy's peyed up?'

'Don't be silly!' She was her own brisk self again. 'Pull yourself together. See—here's Maisie.'

The door opened and a pile of headgear preceded the girl into the kitchen; so many hats had she to control that her father had to remind her to shut the door—which she did with her foot and a bang and a draught of cold air.

'Here you are, Dad.' She guided her miniature Tower of Pisa towards the fireplace. 'This old bowler's pretty mucky, but the grease might keep the heat in. Or would you prefer your new soft hat? Or what about this old Home Guard pixie hood?'

Willie rejected them all with a snort. 'Could ye no' a' brung me ma bunnet when Ah asked ye?'

Sarah had been rummaging in a drawer; she now came

forward, saying, ' Here's the very thing—a Balaclava helmet I've knitted for Matt. See—I'll put it on for you.'

' Heh—mind ma sair throat ! ' When his head emerged from the smother of knitted wool, he was just in time to yell at Peter to shut the door after him. Once again there was the back-swinging foot action, the bang, and the draught of cold air.

' I've got all you want here, Dad,' said Peter. ' GOO to LAB of the *Encyclopaedia* ; The *Twentieth Century Dictionary* and the *Doctor's Book*. Catch ! ' From half-way to the fireplace he threw the last-mentioned, but Willie's hands were slow to come out of the quilt and it landed in the bath of water.

' Eh, ya dumplin' ye ! ' roared the patient, while the others also made suitable exclamations. ' Ach, ye're *aye* throwin' books intae the watter. An' look at the mess ye've made o' the quilt ! '

' Oh dear-dear ! ' wailed Sarah. ' The quilt's soaking. It's enough to give him pneumonia.'

' Pewmonia ! ' burst out Willie, throwing off the besprinkled article. ' Oh ! Ah never thocht o' that.'

When the book was rescued from the water it was found to be very little damaged ; Willie, however, insisted that he would need to be hung up on the pulley along with the quilt as his trousers were—like his handkerchief earlier in the evening— ' wringing.'

' You could have caught the book if you'd tried, Dad ! ' declared Peter.

' Hoo could Ah—an' me no' weel ? '

When another quilt had been fetched and wrapped round him, and while another kettleful of water had been put on to boil, the patient demanded the *Doctor's Book* and his spectacles. Peter, handing the articles over, grumbled that some people didn't half like to be danced attendance upon, and there was some slight huffiness on his father's part because Peter's attitude betokened a certain lack of filial respect. After that there was some delay until the legs of the spectacles had been persuaded to hook themselves through the wool of the helmet and round the ears of the student of amateur specifics. At length, though, Willie was thumbing his way through the catalogue of diseases.

'Whaur are we ? "Colour blindness . . . concussion . . . consumption. . . ." ' He paused, coughed tentatively, and exclaimed, ' *Consumption !* Jeengs, Ah never thocht o' that ! Sarah—d'ye think Ah've maybe got consumption ? '

Sarah dismissed the possibility with a curt ' Don't be silly ! '

' I'd stick to diphtheria, if I were you,' said Maisie. ' I know an awfully nice-looking girl who's nursing in Ruchill.'

' Whit's that ? ' asked Willie with only half his attention ; already he was exploring new avenues of pathological probabilities. ' " Cutting the teeth—dandruff—dip'theria." Here we are ! Whit dis it say ? ' Clearing his throat and swallowing the lump of dread in his gullet, he read, ' " Diphtheria, symptoms of. The disease begins, like so many others, with a feeling of general depression and feverishness." ' He looked, wide-eyed, from one to the other of his attendants. ' Oh help, that's me a'right ! ' He resumed his reading : ' " There is what seems like a cold in the head, a hoarseness, slight difficulty of swallowing." ' Willie paused to swallow once more, and the pace of his reading increased with mounting excitement. ' " Stiffness of the neck and swelling of the glands about the neck and throat." Jings, Serah, see's me doon ma collar aff the mantelpiece tae Ah try it on an' see if ma neck's swelled ! ' Seeing that his wife was showing no signs of obeying his command, he went on with his investigations. ' " When this swelling occurs, send for the doctor without delay." Oh help ! Ah've got dip'theria ! Get the doctor ! Quick ! '

At that Sarah came forward with a glassful of steaming dark red liquid. ' I'll do nothing of the kind ! ' she declared. ' See, here's a black-currant drink. Take it while it's hot.'

' Ah couldnae ! Ah couldnae swally. Peter—away fur the doctor. Staun' back, Maisie—you'll maybe get it aff me ! Oh help ! This is a terrible to-do.'

' Stop your nonsense and drink this up ! I wish Peter had pitched that *Doctor's Book* into the fire instead of into the water ! '

' But Ah'm tellin' ye Ah couldnae swally a drap ! Aw, but wait ! Did it no' say somethin' aboot fever ? Ah—Ah'm a' shiverin' noo.'

'You'd better look up St. Vitus Dance, then,' was Peter's heartless suggestion.

'Don't you staun' there makin' a fule o' me ! If you were as no' weel as me——'

'Willie !' exclaimed Sarah with an edge of exasperation in her voice, ' pull yourself together and drink this !'

'Go on, Dad !' Maisie wheedled as to a fractious child. 'Black currant is supposed to be terribly good for a sore throat !'

'Will it pit away dip'theria, but ?' He seized the tumbler with sudden resolution, gulped down the hot liquid and complained that it was awful wersh. After that he grumbled about the fuss that was created when more water was being added to the tub ; when the quilt was tucked around him once more he demanded, 'See's that *Doctor's Book* again ! Ah don't like the wey Ah'm shiverin'. Maybe it's pewmonia right anuff !' But after a few desultory glances at the pages he decided he was not in a fit condition to continue the investigation of his own case. 'Here, Maisie !' He handed the book over. 'You look it up —ma eyes is waterin' somethin' terrible.'

Maisie thumbed the pages through ' pins and needles ' and ' plague,' ignoring Peter's query as to whether shivering was one of the symptoms of plague. 'Ah, here we are ! "Pneumonia, symptoms of. The first decided symptom of pneumonia will be shortness of breath and there is a stitch in the side." You haven't got that anyway, Dad.'

'Hoo dae *you* know ! Jist because Ah keep my sufferin's tae masel'.'

'Huh !' said Peter with a great deal of emphasis.

'Peter !' snapped Sarah, ' don't talk like that to your father !'

'I never said a word !'

'You looked plenty then.'

'Go on, Maisie !' The interruption came from the depths of the quilt and was delivered in aggrieved tones. 'Whit else does it say aboot pewmonia ?'

'Oh, it says a lot about shortness of breath and all that sort of thing, but I'm quite sure you haven't got pneumonia.'

'Look up malingering,' was Peter's undaunted suggestion.

'Peter ! Don't be vulgar !'

'That wasn't vulgar, Mother !'

'Listen to this, Peter !' exclaimed Maisie ghoulishly. 'It says here that typhus starts with a headache and a coated tongue.'

Willie's eyes opened as well as his mouth. 'Typhus !' he gasped. 'Oh-oh ! Typhus ! Does it say onythin' aboot a bad breath like mine ?'

At that Sarah thought it was time she was taking a firm hold on the situation. 'Peter !' she ordered. 'Away you go down to Mrs. McDruggit. When she was at the door just now complaining about us knocking down on her, she said her husband was ill and she'd sent for the doctor. Tell her to ask the doctor to come up here before he goes away. Maybe he'll put a stop to this nonsense about typhus.'

'Okay.' Peter went out with an air of mock resignation.

'Tell him it's not a matter of life and death,' shouted Maisie after him.

'Eh, ya callous bizzum, ye !' put in the patient. 'An' me maybe at daith's door wi' typhus fever. Get you away oota here an' let me get tae ma bed.'

'With pleasure !' Maisie bounced out of the room and joined her brother in the little hallway. While they were exchanging views on their father's behaviour, Sarah was making a direct statement on the same subject. 'Really, Willie, you're the biggest baby I ever met ! See—there's a towel. Dry your feet while I empty this bath. Just look at the work you're giving me—I'll need to go and put clean sheets on the bed for the doctor coming. And your clean pyjamas are needing mended—I'll have to get you a pair of Peter's.'

'Ach, don't fuss !'

But she did fuss—for a few minutes at least, but the doorbell announcing the doctor's arrival came too soon for her. She met Maisie in the hall and whispered that she wanted a word with the doctor before he saw her father, a device that Maisie understood perfectly.

'Oh, Doctor,' whispered Sarah in a moment or two, 'before you go in to see my husband, I just want to let you know he's never been ill before, and he's inclined to imagine things. To my mind it's nothing but a cold he's got, but maybe you'll manage to talk some sense into him. He's not sure whether it's dip'theria or pneumonia or typhus.'

' So that's the way of it ! ' The doctor exchanged a twinkling smile with the harassed woman. ' Just you leave him to me ! ' He followed Sarah into the kitchen and greeted Willie with a cheerful ' Good-evening, Mr. McFlannel. How are you feeling ? '

' Terrible bad, Doctor.' The voice was feeble. ' Ma heid's sair an' Ah cannae swally.'

' Mn ? Well, just hold this thermometer under your tongue.' While this operation was being performed the doctor asked for a spoon, the finding of which Sarah in turn delegated to Peter. ' And how's the rest of the family ? ' asked the doctor, with one eye on his patient solemnly sucking the thermometer.

' Oh, fine, thanks ! ' said Sarah, delighted at his interest. ' Peter here is an engineer. A radio engineer. He'll maybe be an announcer one of these days.'

Peter's hand was arrested in its fumbling in the spoon-drawer. ' Oh, Mother ! ' he blurted out in shame and protest. ' You know it's not that kind of radio engineering ! '

But Sarah was intent on telling the doctor all about the family. After all, he had asked, hadn't he ! ' Polly's living in Edinburgh, you know. She's married and got a nice wee boy. And Matt's in the Navy.'

' Maisie's teaching, isn't she ? '

' Yes.' She was just about to add something when a mumble from the quilted cocoon at the fireside stopped her.

' I'll relieve you of the thermometer, Mr. McFlannel,' said the doctor. ' What were you saying ? '

' Ah said Ah couldnae get swallyin' ma spittle.' He did so, adding, ' Is—is it serious, Doctor ? '

The doctor shook the thermometer, replaced it, and, declining to answer the question, stripped off the quilt and said, ' I'll listen to your chest now. Just pull up your shirt.'

With a look of apprehension on his face Willie tugged at his shirt, trying to learn his fate from the doctor's face bending down

to fit the stethoscope into his ears. 'Take big breaths,' ordered
the doctor. Willie heaved like a vacuum-cleaner going into
action, and had to be restrained. 'Say ninety-nine,' said the
doctor repeatedly as he dabbed the instrument here and there
over the hairy chest. Still non-committal, he unhitched the
stethoscope from his ears, pulled down Willie's shirt, and told
him to open his mouth. Before he had had time to swallow his
spittle again the invalid was conscious of a cold piece of metal
being laid against his tongue while the doctor flashed his pencil-
torch into his mouth. Resisting the temptation to retch, Willie
held his head up to the light and at the first opportunity asked,
'Is it serious, Doctor?'

Still the judgment was stayed. 'Let me feel your pulse,'
said the doctor.

'Oh my! Ah'm awful no'weel, Doctor!' peched Willie,
yielding up a flabby wrist.

'We had Polly's wee Ian here,' went on Sarah as though she
had never been interrupted. 'He takes after my side of the
family.'

'Can ye no' keep quiet!' barked the patient with sudden
access of strength. 'Hoo can the doctor hear ma pulse if you
keep yatterin' on?'

The doctor straightened himself. 'Well, Mr. McFlannel,' he
pronounced, 'you'll have to take very great care of yourself.
Get into bed straight away.'

'It's serious, then?' asked Willie with grave self-importance.

'You'll need careful feeding.' The doctor was steering a
careful course between the several anxieties of both husband and
wife. 'Nothing but milk puddings, Mrs. McFlannel. And you
might give him a dose of castor oil. Be generous with it.'

Before Sarah could acquiesce Willie rapped out, 'Castor ile!
Milk puddin's! Cuc-could Ah no' get a wee bit fried haddy,
Doctor?'

'Well, haddy if you like, but not fried. And certainly no
chips!'

'Aw, here, Doctor, Ah'm no' near as bad as the wife makes me
oot tae be! D'ye think Ah could get a wee draw at ma pipe?'

'What!' exclaimed the doctor, avoiding Sarah's eye. 'With a throat like yours?'

His partisanship for Sarah's cause was over-emphasized, for it caused Willie to clutch his neck and ask, 'Is—is there no' much hope, Doctor?'

'Now, now, there's no need for you to be worrying about the undertaker yet!' The doctor was bundling his gadgets back into his case. 'Mrs. McFlannel, I'll give you a prescription to send to the chemist, and you'll get some powders. Give him one every four hours—I'm afraid they'll not taste very pleasant.'

While he was writing the necessary form Willie asked when his next visit would be made, and got the answer, spoken rather casually, that as Mr. McDruggit would be requiring another examination the following day, Mr. McFlannel would be inspected in the bye-going.

'Eh, Doctor,' murmured Willie hesitatingly. 'Ah—Ah havenae made ma will yet.'

'Is that so?' The tone was still casual. 'Well, there's no time like the present, you know.' With what seemed to Willie indecent haste, the doctor got himself out of the kitchen, accompanied by Sarah. When the door was closed behind them the patient looked in anguish at his son. 'Heh, Peter—see whit he's written on the certificate.'

Peter made a show of examining the document from various angles, finally holding it up in front of the mirror, a dodge that irritated his father beyond endurance. 'Can ye no' make oot the writin'?'

'No. It looks like "corry-zah." Where's the *Doctor's Book* till I look it up.'

'"Corry-zah,"' repeated Willie. 'Ah wonder if it'll mean an operation?'

Peter found the place at last. 'Ah, here we are! Oh, it should be pronounced "corYza"—you know, to rhyme with "oor Isa."'

'Never mind poetry the noo!' snapped Willie. 'Whit's it say? It must be serious if the doctor's comin' back tae see me the morn.'

'Huh!' Peter's laugh had still the quality of the adolescent hoot. 'It says "Coryza is just another name for a cold in the head"!'

'Whit!' gasped Willie, jumping to his feet and casting his imaginary grave-clothes from him. 'A cauld in the heid! Wait tae Ah get the haud o' that doctor. Here—help me aff wi' this bloomin' helmet.'

He was still struggling with the woolly visor when Sarah came back into the kitchen, saying, 'He's a real nice doctor, that.' When she caught sight of what her husband was up to she remonstrated with him, but in vain.

'A cauld in the heid!' he spluttered when he had won clear of his gag. 'Peter, away doon fur a fish supper wi' a double lota chips. Whaur's ma pipe?' he added defiantly. 'Ony matches, Serah?'

CHAPTER 6

TEA IN THE PARLOUR

A FEW evenings later Willie came home from his work to find the kitchen looking extraordinarily tidy—so much so that there was not even a meal set on the table for him. As was to be expected, he made a flanking attack by way of protest :

'Heh, Serah, whit's up ? Ye're a' dressed up like a dish o' fish.'

Sarah retorted : 'Dear me, do you not remember this is the night Maisie's boy-friend's coming up for tea ? '

'Oh—the Air Force chap we've been hearin' aboot ? '

'Yes—he's a pilot officer or something. So just you hurry up and get dressed before he arrives.'

'Dressed ? Whit fur ? '

'What for ? ' repeated Sarah. 'Do you want to disgrace your daughter by sitting down to tea the way you are ? '

'An' whit-fur no' ? ' Willie's tones were belligerent. 'If ma workin' claes is guid anuff fur Maisie tae take 'er tea wi' every nicht they're guid anuff fur 'er lawd. Ah'm sure the chap's no' comin' tae look at me ! ' As though for comfort he bent down and stroked the shaggy, greying coat of his darling Lassie, now more devoted to him than ever. 'Ony idea whit's fur tea, Lassie ? ' he murmured to the dog. 'D'ye think it'll be ham an' twa eggs ? '

Sarah took up the challenge. 'Ham and eggs ! Of course not ! It's fish custard. Now, for goodness' sake don't you start asking for a second helping before Jim's had some.'

'Jim ? ' queried Willie, examining a thin patch in the dog's coat. 'Wha's Jim ? '

'Oh, stupid ! ' Sarah's exasperation was increased by the fact of her own discomfort over the coming visit. 'Maisie's boy-friend, of course ! ' To be sure, Jim wasn't the first boy-friend Maisie had had, but she, Sarah, had felt it was time she had a look at this fellow who seemed to be more popular than the others. Maisie had protested when the suggestion had been made that he should share a meal with the family, and Sarah was now tasting the rather doubtful sweets of victory in the battle that had ensued. She was old-fashioned, she admitted to herself, but, after all, a mother wanted to know what kind of company her daughter was keeping. She didn't hold with this casual here to-day and gone to-morrow sort of friendships between the sexes, but Maisie's reiteration that Jim and she were just 'good pals' only made her the more irritated now that the visit was only a few minutes distant. She took the opportunity to vent some of her irritation on her husband. 'Here!' she said, 'while I mind—for goodness' sake don't say "Eat up, we're in the Co." or "The mair ye eat the bigger the dividend."'

Willie looked up from his crouching position over the dog. 'Ah don't see ony hairm in that. An' forbye, it's no' a thing Ah'm likely tae say.'

'What! All my married life I've been trying to train you not to say that when folk come to the house, and as sure as death out you come with it!'

'Ach, you! Ah'll soon no' get trampin' on yer corns. Ah'm aye openin' ma mooth an' pittin' ma foot in it accordin' tae you!'

'Well, I only tell you for your own good. There's another thing too. Don't tuck your napkin into your collar.'

'Gi'e me a peenie or a daidly or somethin', then.'

'Can you not lay your napkin on your lap like any other man?'

'Ach, the bloomin' thing'll no' stey on ma knees—it slips aff ontae the floor, an' when Ah rax doon fur it Ah aye bring doon ma teacup efter me.'

'Oh, of course! You can always be relied on to make a mess of things. Come on—hurry up and get cleaned up.'

'Whit time's the chap comin'?'

'He'll be here in five minutes,' said Sarah with some attempt at inaccuracy in a good cause. 'So, for goodness' sake hurry. . . .'

Amazingly Willie got to his feet and made for the bathroom,

colliding *en route* with Maisie who came into the kitchen, saying :

'I think that's everything, Mother. The table's looking very nice.'

'Whit's that ye said, Maisie ? ' demanded Willie, as though the idea had only just occurred to him. ' We're no' ha'ein' wur tea ben the hoose, are we ? '

'Of course we are ! ' snapped Sarah. ' What's the use of having a dining-table and a sideboard in the room if we never use it.'

'Ah thocht ye kep' wur auld claes in the sideboard,' murmured Willie.

'Oh, don't waste time ! '

Willie moved towards the bathroom once again, but once again his progress was arrested, this time by the determination to score off his wife. ' Ah think ye're daft—the pair o' ye ! Giein' the chap a wrang impression.'

'In what way, Dad ? ' inquired Maisie, taking sides with her mother.

Before Willie could reply, Sarah got in with, ' We couldn't give anybody a wrong impression as long as you're there to give the show away ! '

'D'ye tell me that ! ' he sneered.

'Oh, Dad,' put in Maisie, ' I wonder if you'd do me a special favour ? '

'Ach, whit next ? ' He abandoned his search for the bathroom and made for the sink in the scullery, demanding to know what he had done to deserve such a tortured life at the hands of his ambitious womenfolk.

'Will you *please* not tell him that hoary old story about the boiled bacon ? '

'Whit story aboot whit b'iled bacon ? ' he asked, well aware that this ground had already been covered several times previously on similar occasions.

'Oh, you know the one about the old man who's dying——'

'Oh, that yin ! ' he exclaimed, just as if his memory had only then been refreshed, ' Ah'd forgotten a' aboot hit.'

' And Dad——' continued the girl.

' Whit ? '

' Don't eat with your knife and don't——' but the rest of her
instructions were lost in the commotion caused by Lassie barking
her welcome to Peter, by Willie running the water to drown her
' don'ts ' and by Sarah's torrent of abuse directed at Peter for
being late—' to-night of all nights ! '

Peter, in mystification, wanted to know if there was a ' do ' on.

' Ay ! ' shouted Willie from the scullery. ' Maisie's lawd's
comin' up fur tae inspect the faimly. An' we're tae ha'e wur
tea in the parlour.'

' Ugh ! ' grumbled Peter.

' Put on your new suit, Peter,' coaxed Sarah. ' You look
awfully smart in it.'

' No bloomin' fear ! What'll *he* be wearing, Maisie ? '

' Why—his uniform, of course ! '

' Well, my dongarees are *my* uniform, see ? If you want me
to doll myself up I could put on my firewatcher's helmet and
gas-mask. And Dad could put on his Home Guard tunic.'

' You're jealous ! ' snapped Maisie who also was feeling the
strain of the occasion. She was not too sure of her attitude
towards Jim, being afraid that this fuss might make him jump
to the conclusion that she was eager for a more official basis to
their friendship. Sarah cut into the girl's obvious desire for an
argument.

' Will you two stop quarrelling and clear out of the kitchen.
Your father's going to change his suit.'

' Ah tell ye whit,' said Willie, advancing with a towel in his
hands, ' jist gi'e me an' Peter wur tea at the jawbox.'

' Oh, Dad ! ' wailed Maisie, ' can you not say " sink " instead
of jawbox ? It would be less work ! '

At that moment the door-bell rang and it was Sarah's turn to
wail. ' Oh dear-dear ! ' she cried. ' He's here before his time ! '

' And we're not ready ! ' whimpered Maisie apprehensively.
' Oh, I wish we'd just had the tea in the kitchen here after all !
I could have taken him into the sitting-room till Dad and Peter
were dressed.'

'Away you go to the door,' urged her mother, 'and I'll try and make these two be as quick as they can.'

Maisie went out expressing the fervent wish that she had never asked the fellow to come to the house. She turned back to say, 'Dad—you'll remember, won't you ! He's . . . terribly . . .' she searched for the right word. 'I mean, he's such a . . . Oh, you know what I mean !' she implored.

'Ay !' said Willie. 'Ah ken fine, lass. He's a toff an' Ah'm jist a common five-eighth.'

'Stop your nonsense, Willie !' commanded Sarah, then, pushing Maisie towards the outside door, she followed the girl and shut the kitchen door after them.

Left alone with his father, Peter whispered, 'I say, Dad, what about you and me doing a bunk as soon as they've taken him into the sitting-room ?'

'The very dab ! In hauf a meenit they'll be tellin' us fur tae pit on wur lum hats an' claw-haimmer jaikets.' For a moment or two the pair of them eyed each other as if sizing up their respective capacities for trickery ; they listened to the noises that came from the hall—voices of welcome and introduction and effusion, footsteps going in the direction of the sitting-room, and finally the shutting of a door. 'Are ye ready, son ?' growled Willie. But before they could make any move, the door of the kitchen opened and Maisie walked in on their chagrin.

'Dad !' she whispered, not noticing their embarrassment, 'I just slipped back to ask you if you won't try—*please* to speak English.'

'Speak English !' repeated the aggrieved Willie. 'Jeengs, Ah don't ken ony ither langwidge.' Clearing his throat he proceeded to show his linguistic abilities in a high falsetto tone : '"Good-evening, Jeem. What glawrious weathah we're heving faw this tehm of the yah." Hoo'll that dae, Maisie ?'

In spite of herself Maisie had started to giggle. 'Oh, Dad, you're the limit !' she exclaimed. 'But you don't need to work at it as hard as all that !' Then, turning to Peter, she added, 'Oh, Peter, for goodness' sake, will you not shovel down your food like a pig ?'

'I didn't know pigs could use shovels,' retorted Peter.

'Oh, don't try to be funny!' she wheedled. 'I *do* want Jim to get a good impression of the family.'

'Here,' suggested Willie, bending down and lifting up the dog at his feet. 'Take Lassie. She barks wi' a Kelvinside accent.'

Maisie was on the point of going out in disgust and disappointment, when Peter called after her, 'I wouldn't put my shirt on the chance of Lassie creating a good impression with her Kelvinside bark. After all, what about the noise she makes when she drinks out of a saucer!'

'Oh, you're hopeless, the pair of you!' she flung over her shoulder.

In a moment or two the sitting-room door had closed, and Willie whispered, 'That's hur away, Peter. Are ye comin'? The road's clear.' He paused to reassure himself, but the sitting-room door opened again and, before they had time even to test the hiding capacity of the kitchen press, Sarah was with them, exclaiming:

'Come on, you two. Are you never dressed yet? Peter—go away and take off those dongarees and put on a clean collar. And don't leave the bathroom like a pigsty.'

Slamming out of the kitchen, Peter mumbled, 'Huh—so you think I'm a pig too!'

'What did he mean by that?' asked Sarah.

But Willie ignored the question and asked another that was nearer his heart, 'Whit's Maisie's lawd like?'

'He seems nice enough. Awful Englified, of course, so for goodness' sake try to speak proper.'

'Ach, lea'e me alane. Ah'm jist fair scunnered wi' this everlastin' tellin' me tae speak proper.'

'Well, it's your own fault!' Sarah spoke with only half her attention, for she was trying to concentrate on the problems of plates being warm enough, fish being cooked enough and the kettle being full enough.

Willie, making a token change in his raiment by the simple expedient of turning his collar outside-in, asked diffidently, 'D'ye think—it's—serious this time?'

'How should I know ? Girls never tell their mothers anything these days. Anyway, Maisie's fancied herself in love dozens of times.'

'Love !' Willie contemplated his reflection as he gave a final tug to his tie. 'Ma auld faither used tae say love wis a yuckiness in at the hert ye cannae get in tae claw.' Presumably pleased with what he saw in the mirror, he turned round to his wife. 'Heh, Serah, hoo'm Ah lookin' ? In ma clean collar, Ah mean ?'

'Fine,' said Sarah without checking up on her statement. 'Now don't bother me while I'm making the tea.'

'If Ah wis a younger man, wid ye mairry me again ?'

'Will you stop talking nonsense !' The remark was more of a command than a request. 'See—help me to carry this stuff into the sitting-room. Now mind—don't shake hands with him as if you were cawing a wringer, and don't gobble up your food before anybody else, and don't——'

Willie cut her short with his perennial injunction to 'cheer up, she never died a winter yet.' As he shuffled himself into his jacket again he asked what particular article she wished him to carry.

'The plates that are warming on top of the stove,' she told him. 'Now for goodness' sake be careful with them and don't let them drop.'

But they had dropped before she had finished speaking, Willie meanwhile yelling that his fingers had been scorched.

'You clumsy footer, you !' wailed Sarah in distress. 'Three plates in smithereens !'

'Well, hoo wis Ah tae know they were scaudin' hot ?' demanded Willie, blowing his finger-tips while Sarah reached into the coal-bunker for a shovel and brush to sweep up the wreckage. He hovered over her in awkward though dumb apology, calling forth, thereby, another complaint.

'Here—get out of my road ! I could flype you, so I could !'

'Whit aboot ma sair fing-ers, but ?'

'Oh, don't be a baby !' The brush did its work efficiently. 'I'll have to put plain plates at the bottom of the pile.'

As if to make amends Willie assured her that she didn't need to give him a plate to match, adding, ' Ah can sup ma share oota that camisole thing.'

' Oh, you would ! And anyway, it's a casserole, not a camisole—so don't you be giving us a red face by calling it the wrong thing in front of Jim.' Disposing of the breakages, she inserted three cold plates at the bottom of the pile and gave it to her husband with the assurance that he would not be scalded this time. The other necessaries were assembled on a tray. ' Are you ready ? ' she asked.

' Ay. Oh ay. Lead on, Macduff ! ' At that moment Peter appeared, and his services were immediately requisitioned to carry the teapot. There was a murmur added to the effect that Jim would be horrified when he discovered that the McFlannels didn't possess a tea-trolley, but it was an arrow that missed its mark for Willie merely retorted :

' Ach, ye should a' had the tea in the kitchen an' nane o' this palaver.'

Sarah paused in the procession to turn on her husband. ' Has it not dawned on you that we're trying to put our best foot forward for Maisie's sake ? Jim's a real gentleman, so he is ! '

' Dad ! ' said Peter, in league with his father, ' was there not a villain in the pictures called Gentleman Jim ? '

Once again Sarah paused. ' Peter ! ' she exclaimed. ' Don't say things like that ! Now, Willie, will you remember all that I've told you ? Do try to behave yourself—for Maisie's sake.'

' Ach, come on. Let's get it ower afore Ah take the bo——"

Before the synonym for scunner had left his lips Sarah had got out a warning ' Willie ! '

' Well, afore Ah drop thae plates ! ' he amended.

' Come on, then ! '

As they passed the outside door *en route* for the sitting-room, Peter made the whispered suggestion that they could slip out then, but his father had lost his zest for intrigue. ' Naw,' said he. ' Come on an' see whit he's like.'

The next minute they were in the room that was called the sitting-room by Sarah, the lounge by Maisie, the pawrlur by

Willie, my room by Peter; it might with equal justification have been called the dining-room, for a sideboard and dining-table formed its most prominent features. Peter slept in it, but his bed was concealed behind a door.

'Well, here we are!' announced Sarah unnecessarily. 'Jim, this is Dad.'

The young man in the uniform of the Royal Air Force stepped forward, saying in a mincing voice, 'How d'you do, Mr. McFlehnnel.'

'Pleased tae meet ye,' declared Willie, extending his right hand and hugging the pile of plates to his bosom with his left. Out of pity for the young man whose hand was being used like a pump-handle, Sarah seized the plates and said:

'Jim, this is Peter.'

'How d'you,' said the pilot officer feebly.

'Fine, thanks,' responded Peter, in defiance of Maisie's instructions. 'How's yourself?'

Sarah began sorting everybody out. 'Willie, you go to the top of the table. Jim, will you sit at this side, and Maisie and Peter over there. The weather's been awful for this time of the year, hasn't it?'

'Yes, it has,' agreed the visitor with more courtesy than accuracy, but his lapse went unnoticed in the commotion that followed his tramping on Lassie's tail.

'Heh, Lassie!' called Willie, on the defensive at once. 'Come on up here aside me. An' if ye're guid Ah'll gie ye a wee bit o' ma fish.'

'Now, Willie!' put in Sarah, anxious to put a face on things, 'you know what I've said over and over again about giving that dog scraps off the table.'

Peter was the last to sit down. He did so with the observation that it wasn't good for a dog to get more than one meal a day.

'It's not the dog I'm thinking about,' said his mother. 'It's the carpet.' At that moment she discovered she had forgotten to bring a slop basin, so Maisie was dispatched to fetch it.

Some imp of mischief took hold of Willie. He looked with

silent contempt at the monument of refinement that was his guest, then broke out with, 'If we'd had wur tea in the kitchen the same as usual, ye wouldnae of needed a slop basin. Ye could justa syned the cups oot at the jawbox in the scullery.'

Sarah decided to ignore the remark by asking if the visitor took sugar, but it appeared that he took neither sugar nor milk. The information was imparted in such genteel speech that Willie's imp possessed and controlled him again.

'Heh, Serah, whit's this big hankie fur?' He held up his fancily-folded napkin. 'Ah cannae blaw ma nose wi't. It's as hard as a board.'

Hoping that Maisie's return would cover the incident, Sarah whispered fiercely that it was his napkin, then turning to Maisie she suggested, 'I tell you what—you pour out the tea while I dish up the fish.'

Matters proceeded quietly for a few minutes till a plateful of fish was passed to the guest with the remark about the weather being awful for the time of the year. The visitor accepted the plate while agreeing with the conversational gambit. He added:

'Do you want me to pess this up to Mr. McFlehnnel?'

'Oh, that'll no' be fur me!' Willie assured him. 'There's ower much there. They never gie me onythin' but the scrapin's o' the pot.'

'Oh, Dad!' protested Maisie.

'Don't pay any attention to him, Jim,' said Sarah. 'It's for yourself—I hope it'll be all right. I've been getting out of the way of making fish custards these days.' But Jim was too obtuse to notice the implication that the family were having a treat in his honour; in any case Peter was asking him a question.

'Do you do much flying these days?'

'Not much. Are you—interested in flehing?'

'I'll say I am!' replied Peter with emphasis. 'I wanted to join the Air Force but the firm wouldn't release me.'

'Peter's a radio engineer, Jim!' observed Sarah. 'He'll maybe be an announcer one of these days.'

'Mother!' The affronted rebuke came from the maligned radio engineer. 'The last time you said that, I told you——'

'Ach, keep yer hair on,' called Willie in consolation from the top of the table. 'Ehm, Sarah, Ah don't suppose Ah'll get saucerin' ma tea the night?'

If the remark was intended to draw attention away from Peter it was certainly successful, for Sarah gaped at him.

'Saucering your tea!' she exclaimed. 'I never saw you doing that in your life!' What, she wondered, was the matter with him to-night? He could usually be depended on to put his foot in things, but never quite so badly as this. Her astonishment must have reproached him, for he explained:

'Ach, Ah jist meant—suppose Ah wis in the habit o' saucerin' ma tea—Ah widnae get daein' it the night.'

'Jim,' said Sarah, trying to keep calm, 'will you have white bread or brown?'

'Oh, brahn, eef you please.'

Once again Willie contemplated the exceeding gentility of his daughter's boy friend; the result was that he fell once again into the hands of the imp of his own mischief. 'Eat up, Jim,' he said. 'We're in the Co., ye know. The mair ye eat, the bigger the dividend!'

'Oh, Dad!' Maisie's voice seemed on the edge of tears.

Sudden hope comforted Sarah. 'I—ehm—I suppose it'll be terribly difficult for you English to make out what us Scotch folk are saying, Jim?'

'Well, of course, Eh——' began Jim, when he was interrupted.

'Here!' exclaimed Willie, 'that reminds me. Did ye ever hear the story o' the——'

'Get on with your tea, Willie!' came the command from the opposite end of the table. Really, he was beyond all bounds to-night. What *would* Jim think? Sarah looked at her daughter and exchanged pity for vexation.

'Have some more tea, Dad,' said the girl.

'Ah havenae touched whit ye gien me a'readies.' He went on remorselessly, 'As Ah wis sayin'—did ye ever hear the story o' the Englishman——'

Peter nudged his sister. 'Thank heaven it's a new one, Maisie.'

'The Englishman,' persisted Willie, 'that wis traivellin' in the hielans. He came across a crood like an execution in yin o' thae wee villages at the back o' beyond. So up he goes tae an auld wife an' asks 'er whit's up. "Ach," says she, "it's jist a wee wean that's coupit intae a byne o' saepy sapple, but she's comin' tae noo."'

Jim giggled. 'Well, thet's a new one on me, Mr. McFlehnnel.'

'Ay but d'ye unnerstaun' it ? There's hardly an English word in the hale story.'

'Never heed him, Jim,' advised Sarah. 'Pass the butter up to your father, Peter.'

'Huh,' said Willie, reaching out his knife, 'high jinks the nicht if it's butter. It's a wonder ye havenae got a wee dish o' mary-jane doon just fur me alane.'

Maisie sighed. Was there ever a father like this ? Just how long would Jim stand for it ? What could he be thinking ? How was Mother able to endure that sort of thing year in and year out ? 'Peter,' she said, 'could you not tell Jim about the work you're doing ? With you being in the radio line the two of you might have quite a lot in common.'

'Eh'm sure we have, Petah !' declared Jim, rising to the occasion, and gaining a point in his favour. 'What kehnd of wirk are you tehning out ?'

'Oh, it's very hush-hush, you know,' said Peter evasively. 'I'll tell you all about it after tea.'

'Jim,' asked his hostess, 'is your fish custard to your taste all right ?'

'It's ebsolutely wizard, Mrs. McFlehnnel.'

'Aw here, that's a shame !' complained the host. 'Could ye no' 've seen the chap got a decent bit fish ?'

'But it is !' protested Jim. 'It's simply spiffing !'

'Ah thocht ye said it wis wizened !'

'Wizard, Dad !' whispered Maisie, blushing vicariously, 'not wizened.'

Peter thought it was time to lend a hand in obliterating his father's influence, so he offered to let Jim see a wireless set he had made himself. 'After tea, of course,' he added.

'I thought this was the night you usually went out with Bob McLeather,' said Maisie.

'Ugh, it's not all that important!' said Peter.

'You'll meet Bob McLeather to-night—as usual!' declared his mother firmly. Young couples, she felt, had to get to know each other, and what better place for that than the girl's own home? Willie, however, had different ideas.

'Ach away wi' ye, Serah, are ye no' gonnae let Peter gie's a wee choon on 'is fiddle? Ah thocht this wis a pairty!' As no-one took up his suggestion he finished his portion of fish and then demanded more, with the observation, 'A' Ah got ye coulda seen wi' yae blin' e'e an' the ither yin stuffed wi' rags,' a remark that caused Sarah to express inward gratitude for the fact that Jim, being what she called 'an Englishman, poor soul,' wouldn't understand.

'There's no more fish!' she said aloud.

'Have ye nae spam in the hoose, then? Or b'iled bacon?'

'I've no boiled bacon,' said Sarah wearily, 'but if you're as hungry as all that——'

'Here,' exclaimed Willie, his hunger apparently forgotten, 'b'iled bacon! That reminds me—did ye ever hear the story, Jim——'

Maisie rushed in with, 'Oh, Dad, there's a wee play on the wireless to-night——'

Sarah tried to side-track the chestnut by announcing that she had something special in the oven to follow the fish course, but Peter growled:

'Oh, let him tell it. He won't be happy till he gets it out of his system.'

'Eh'd lehk to hear it, Mr. McFlehnnel,' said the visitor politely, so politely, in fact, that his Sassenachity was borne to his hostess on relieving wings, and she sighed:

'Well, thank goodness, you being English you won't make out half of it.'

'It's aboot an auld chap that wis deein', see?'

'He means, Jim,' explained Maisie, 'that the story's about an old man who was dying.'

' So Eh gethered.   Yes, Mr. McFlehnnel ? '

' Well, 'e wis lyin' in the kitchen bed, see ?   So 'e keeks oot an' sees a dollop o' b'iled bacon on the dresser.   Then 'e heaves a sigh, an' 'is wife says wis there onythin' 'e'd like.   " Ay," says he, "Ah wid like fine tae hae a wee puckle o' thon b'iled bacon." " Ye cannae get that," says the wife, " *that's fur yer funeral* ! " '

' Jahlly good ! ' sniggered Jim.

' Oh, Willie ! ' wailed Sarah, recognizing the insincerity of the snigger, ' I don't know what makes you persist in telling that story.   Here—watch !   Your cuff's trailing in the butter dish ! '

' Ach, well, that shows Ah'm no' used wi' eatin' wi' ma jaiket on.   Ah'll jist take it aff ! ' he declared obligingly.

' Oh, Dad ! '   It was Maisie's turn to wail.   ' Please don't ! You know you promised to behave yourself.'

' An' am Ah no' ? ' he queried.

' Willie ! '   Sarah got to her feet with sudden resolution. ' I've got a special treat for you.   A dumpling !   I'm just going to take it out of the oven now.'

The ruse was successful ; the host's attempts to take off his jacket were arrested, while he rubbed his hands, saying, ' Boys-a-boys !   Ah havenae tasted dumplin' fur donkey's ages.   Ye're in fur a treat, Jim.   Wi' you bein' English ye'll no' have tasted dumplin' afore.'

Jim appeared to be making some sort of amendment to this statement, but it was lost in Maisie's fussing over the removal of his fish plate in preparation for the arrival of the dumpling which Sarah had gone to fetch.   ' Would you care to have a pancake ? ' she asked.

' Pancake ! ' put in Willie.   ' It's gettin' its pairty name the night !   We usually ca' it a flannel biscuit.'

Jim accepted the tea-bread, with a courteous murmur about its tasting as sweet by any name, and Willie wondered all over again what could be the attraction in this tailor's dummy that Maisie could be such a fool as to be interested in him.   He felt vaguely disappointed in his daughter ; but a matter of more importance soon dispelled his worries.

71

'Peter!' he whispered, 'while yer mother's away ben the hoose, pit that camisole thing on the floor fur Lassie tae lick.'

'Camisole?' Peter gaped self-consciously at Maisie. 'Oh, you mean casserole!' He was putting the dish on the floor when his mother came back into the room. She caught the manœuvre.

'Peter!' she warned. 'You know quite well I don't like the dog to use the same dishes as ourselves.'

'Ach away, Serah,' grumbled her husband, 'the dug'll no' be as easy pooshuned as a' that. Let 'er have it, Peter. Ony luckies in the dumplin', Serah?'

'No!' She carried the steaming dumpling tenderly to the table, then, noticing that Jim was still occupied in a lady-like way with the pancake, she decided to place it by the fire to await his readiness. Willie, jumping forward to assist her, bungled his movements so badly that he only succeeded in getting in her way, with the melancholy result that the dumpling tottered on its throne. They both tried to save it from falling but it fell just the same, their clutching hands helping to decimate it. Sarah shrieked accusingly, Maisie jumped up to prevent some of the stuff falling on her new frock, Willie yelled with rage and mortification, Lassie barked, Peter shouted on her to be quiet, and even the guest got to his feet.

'It's all your fault!' Sarah pointed an accusing finger at her husband, and from him to the mess on the carpet. 'You're a gowk, so you are! My lovely dumpling! Ruined! Absolutely ruined!'

The pilot officer came round the table to the scene of the accident. Something had happened to him—he looked all at once quite alive. 'Oh, I say,' he said, 'let's all take our spoons and lift some on to our plates. The carpet's perfectly clean—it won't do us any harm. And the dumpling looks wizard.' He got down on his knees.

Sarah blinked at him. My, what a change—he seemed quite a nice fellow after all. And what was that he had said about the dumpling?

'Come on, boys! Muck in!' ordered Willie getting down beside the pilot officer.

' To hang with plates ! ' said Peter from the same position. He was pushing the crumbs into his mouth with such enthusiasm that only he had any idea of what he was saying. ' It's the best dumpling you've ever made, Mother ! Yum-yum ! Look at Lassie ! She's got hold of a bit and it's too hot for her ! '

Even Maisie was amused by the antics of the dog, who was now attempting to throw bits of dumpling up into the air as though to cool them.

' Heh, Lassie,' called Willie in great good humour, ' can ye no' blaw on it ? Or take aff yer bunnet an' waff it ? '

The social atmosphere had warmed up at last ; the whole family were on their knees—the ladies and the guest eating more or less daintily with spoons, while the host and his son used more direct methods.

' Jolly good dumpling, Mrs. McFlehnnel ! ' declared Jim speaking with his mouth full. ' Just the job ! '

' Ay,' said Sarah, her inhibitions falling from her one by one in the informality of the occasion, ' but Ah didnae mean us to be eatin' it on our hunkers.'

Jim was quick to notice the change in her speech. ' Ugh ! ' said he, ' to hang wi' spoons. Fingers were made afore cutlery ! '

Maisie gaped. ' Jim ! You spoke Scotch just now ! '

' Well, and what-for-no' ? Ah was born an' brought up in Motherwell ! '

They all stopped eating to stare at him. So he was human after all—not just a sissy with a handlebar moustache ! The last vestiges of his Kelvinside accent were gone when he confessed, in reply to Willie's query about his ' pan-loaf talk ' :

' Well, ye see, Ah wanted to kind of make a good impression wi' Maisie's fam'ly. Ah was kind of scared of ye all.' He eased his collar. ' Here ! This is warm work ! Ah'm sweatin' ! Whi'd'ye say if we a' take off wur jaikets, Mr. McFlannel ? '

The men took off their jackets and the ladies sucked their fingers. They were at home with one another at last. Maisie, alone, was left with a slightly uneasy feeling. In her heart of hearts she preferred speech that had in it the genteel tinkle of the Kelvin to that which savoured of the broad gurliness of the Clyde.

73

CHAPTER 7

UP IN THE MORNING EARLY

IN spite of the fuel shortage, and as if in corroboration of Willie's philosophy of life, the McFlannels did not succumb to the winter. The spring saw Matt home for an extended leave—a Matt who was becoming increasingly free from his early inhibitions. Maisie, trying to get at the reason for the change, had to be content with the explanation that he was meeting all sorts of chaps in the Navy, but the real cause lay in the fact that Matt was finding self-expression in the short stories he was sending to appreciative editors on both sides of the Atlantic. Some day he was going to surprise his family with a book, but that was a long way off yet. Summer saw the family taking their 'staggered' holidays one by one, with no sign of the ending of queues for Sarah or of the standing-down of the Home Guard for Willie; the war meandered on towards D-day, but in the late autumn of 1943 D-day was still a long way off. Sarah's patience, like that of Hitler, was becoming exhausted. Early one morning she wakened feeling very sorry for herself—there was so much to worry her; and she made the most of each individual item as she turned it over, slowly and anxiously, in her mind. There was Matt, of course, always Matt. How long would it be before a telegraph boy handed in bad news? For a few minutes she wallowed in the grief she was sure was waiting for her round the corner. Then there was the ceaseless business of running the house, the remorselessness of it, the thanklessness; she dusted the furniture faithfully every day, but nobody commended her for her efforts. There was the shopping with its niggardly results; there was the never-ending mending. All of a sudden she felt utterly unable to cope with things one more day. She was tired—she would rest. This extraordinary decision reached, she lay and waited almost gleefully for the ringing of the alarm bell of the clock on the mantelpiece well out of the reach of a sleepy arm.

At seven o'clock the kitchen reverberated to the jangle from the mantelpiece. It was one of the type of alarm clocks which go on ringing until stopped by the pressing of a button ; when this one had rung for twenty seconds and Sarah had made no move to get up, Willie stirred in his sleep and grunted :

'Heh, Serah, the alarm !'

'I hear it !' she told him calmly.

'Are ye no' gonnae get up an' pit it aff?'

'No.'

The man raised a tousled head and looked at her. 'Whit ! Ye're no' gonnae. . . . Here, whit's up wi' ye ?'

'Nothing.'

'Get up, well, an' stop that racket ! Ye'll ha'e Mrs. McMuslin knockin' doon on ye.'

Now for it ! 'Get up yourself,' she said.

'Eh?' The man was wide awake and aghast with astonishment.

'You heard me.'

'B—but it's you that gets up first every mornin' ! Ye've been daein' it a' wur mairrit life.'

'Yes—so it's time I had a change.'

Willie sat up and glowered at the clamant clock. 'Here, fur the luva mike pit aff that alarm !'

'Put it off yourself. You're nearer it than I am.'

'Serah, are ye ill or whit ?'

'I'm fine !'

'Then whit the bleezes is up wi' ye ?' He was never at his best when he wakened in the morning, but he seemed worse than ever on the present occasion. Sarah wondered for a moment if he were going to shake her ; instead, he shook himself on to the floor and made a dive at the offensive tintinnabulation, attacking it with malice aforethought. In the silence that followed he demanded once more, 'Noo, whit's up wi' ye ? Is't a long lie ye want ?'

'No. I'm going to take the day in bed, that's all.'

His amazement made him inarticulate. At last he blurted out, 'The day in bed ! On a Monday ? Washin' day ? Here, Serah, ye must hae a slate loose !'

'No, I'm just tired. I want a day in bed when I've got the health and strength to enjoy it.'

'The health an' strength ! Ah never heard sich rubbish.'

'Well, my mind's made up, so you may as well——'

'Help ma boab, wumman, whit aboot wur breakfasts ? An' wur pieces fur wur dinner ? An' the hoose ? An' the week's washin' ? Tae say nothin' aboot whit the wife next door'll say if ye havenae got the stair swep' ! '

'I don't care ! '

'Here ! ' He made a grab at his trousers. 'Ah better go fur the doctor. Are ye sure ye havenae got a pain somewhere ? '

'Quite sure ! '

'Here, let me feel if ye're fevered ! Yer face is gey red.' But she turned her head away from his exploratory hand. 'Wid Ah no' be better fur tae shout fur Maisie ? '

'You can shout for Maisie if you like. She'll need all her time if she's to make the breakfast and your pieces—although why you and Peter can't make your own pieces beats me to know. Now will you leave me alone ? '

The sheer audacity of her penultimate statement shook Willie. 'Aw, heh, Serah, fun's fun, but tae hang wi' chappin' on a blin' man's tinny ! '

'You hurry up or you'll be late for your work ! '

'Ah'm hurryin' as fast as Ah can—oot fur the doctor ! '

'But I don't need a doctor ! '

Willie struggled with his night and day raiment, murmuring, 'Ah never heard sich nonsense—wantin' tae lie in yer bed jist because ye've got the health an' strength tae enjoy it. Whaur's ma socks ? ' The murmur rose to a shout as he repeated his query,' Whaur's ma socks ? '

'On the floor, likely.'

'. . . So they are ! This is a terrible-like cairry-on in the mornin' an' me rushin' oot tae ma work. Could ye no' 've tellt me last night ? ' In his haste he dealt rather roughly with one of his socks, with the inevitable result. 'Och, tae hang ! Whaur'll Ah get anither pair ? '

'In the top drawer of the chest there. It's awful to think

you've been married for about thirty years and you don't know where your socks are kept. It's high time I went on strike ! '

An idea struck the man. ' D'ye no' think a wee cuppy tea wid help ye ? '

' Oh, I can get a cup of tea when the rest of you are having yours. I made the porridge last night, so you've only got to heat it up. You'd better put the kettle on just now.'

Willie tried wheedling. ' But if Ah made ye a wee cup the noo, maybe it wid help ye tae rise.'

' Never you mind me ! You'll need all your time. I don't want anything to eat anyway. I was reading in the paper the other day that it does your system good to have a day's starvation.'

' A day's starvation ! ' Once again the man peered at his wife. ' Ma conscience—whit next ! Ehm . . . ye havenae a pain or a queer feelin' somewhere ? '

' I have not ! ' There was a touch of hysteria in the cry, ' Oh for pity's sake will you leave me alone ? '

' It's a'right, lass ! ' said Willie soothingly, as if to humour a fractious child. ' Ah'll hae the doctor here afore ye can say Jack Robe'son. Jist you lie quiet there an' don't worry. Is the sun in yer eyes ? Will Ah draw doon the blind ? '

' No-no ! I'm not dead yet ! You hurry up and never mind the doctor. You'll be late for your work.'

' Ah'm thinkin' Ah'd maybe better take the mornin' off. . . . Here, whaur's ma shirt ? '

' Over the back of that chair,' she pointed.

Willie reached for the shirt that had been in full view all the time, and as he shuffled into it he suggested :

' Peter could take a message tae ma manager tellin' 'im whit wey Ah'm no' at ma work the day.' Disregarding Sarah's objections to this procedure, he went on to demand where she had planked his collar stud.

' Look in the coal bunker,' proposed she with heavy sarcasm. ' It's as likely to be there as anywhere else.'

Willie, however, mistook the sarcasm for a sign of mental derangement. ' It's a'right, lass,' he said affectionately. ' Ah'm hurryin' fur the doctor as fast as Ah can. Wid ye like a hot bag ? '

Fumbling beneath the bedclothes at the foot of the bed he added, ' Is yer feet cauld ? '

Sarah shrieked. ' Ya ! Your hands are as cold as ice ! *Will you leave me alone !* '

' Ah'm sorry.' Humbled, frightened, aware of his own gaucherie, he offered to knock up Maisie.

' Put on the kettle first,' said Sarah in such a normal voice that he hastened to obey. She shouted after him, ' The matches are on the shelf above the cooker ! '

' Ah'm no' wantin' matches the noo,' he called back. ' Ah've nae time fur smokin' ma pipe.'

' I meant matches for lighting the gas ! '

There was a touch of hysteria in the tones that brought Willie scuttling back to the bedside once more. ' It's a'right, lass. The gas is lighted. Noo jist you keep quiet ! There's nae need tae get excited.'

' I'm not excited.' As if to emphasize her calmness she closed her eyes, and Willie, after another scared peer at her, proceeded to the door of Maisie's bedroom, whereon he knocked with fanatical zeal and Sarah smiled as she heard him yell :

' Maisie ! Get up quick ! Yer mother's ta'en ill ! Ah'm away oot fur the doctor ! ' A moment later she heard him with less ceremony open the door of the sitting-room and repeat the statement to Peter with even more zeal and less accuracy, for he added the gratuitous information that ' she's lyin' at daith's door ! Hurry ! '

Returning to the kitchen he trod, unslippered, on his collar stud, so sparing Sarah the necessity of telling him to look for it in the jelly pan. His tie, however, eluded his perfunctory glance. ' Heh, Serah, have ye ony idea whaur ma tie is ? '

Without opening her eyes Sarah said, ' It's in front of your nose—look—on the mantelpiece.'

' Okay, Okay. Don't get het-up. It'll be bad fur ye.'

' I'm not in the least het-up. I'm going to turn my back on you, and let you guddle along the best way you can.'

As she heaved round Willie called, ' Heh, jist a meenit ! Whaur's ma collar noo ? '

The reply came back muffled by blankets so that he had to ask her to repeat it—an experiment that he regretted he had inaugurated, for she heaved round again, sat up, and almost spat the words at him, ' I said—look for it ! '

' Ay, but whaur ? In a drawer or whit ? '

' I laid it out for you last night. It's on the table there ! ' She lay down again, saying, ' But would it not be better for you to wash yourself before you put it on ? '

' Ah'll wash masel' efter Ah've brung the doctor ! Here— Ah'll never mind a collar, Ah'll jist pit on a muffler—if Ah can find yin.' He was on the point of asking her guidance on the matter when he thought better of it ; in any case he trod on something else that jagged his feet, and he bethought him of his boots. Ah, there they were, nestling on the treadle of the sewing machine ; he grabbed them with an air of triumph, then let out a howl of disappointment. ' Ach, thae's ma scuffin' buits ! Heh, Serah, whaur's ma ither yins ? '

It was the last straw. Flinging aside the bedclothes, Sarah cried *accelerando, sforzando, crescendo*, ' Oh, whaur's-ma-whaur's-ma-whaur's-ma ! I can't stand it any longer. I'm getting up ! '

Willie rushed to her side and tried to push her back among the blankets again. ' Lie doon, hen,' said he gently. ' Ah'll hae the doctor here in five meenits if Ah've tae yank 'im oot 'is bed.'

Sarah struggled. ' I don't need the doctor ! There's nothing wrong with me ! '

' Then whit the heck d'ye mean by lyin' there kiddin' on ye wur at daith's door fur ? ' There was a tinge of relief in his indignation.

' Be quiet ! Hand me over my dressing-gown—it's at the back of the door there."

' But Ah thocht ye wur—— '

' Oh, forget it ! Away and give Maisie and Peter another shout. Tell them they'll be late for their work.'

' Ach, they can sleep their brains intae train ile fur a' Ah care !' He handed over the dressing-gown like a man in the huff as he

79

added, 'Ye gied me an awful fright the noo—you an yer day's in bed.'

'Some of these days I'll go away a holiday and let you all look after yourselves. You'd maybe appreciate what's done for you if you were left alone for a bit.'

'Ma conscience, wumman, ye'll be greetin' fur a spade an' pail next ! Ah still think Ah should rin fur the doctor !'

Sarah girded herself with the belt of the dressing-gown as she stared at the alarm clock. 'Oh dear-dear ! Look at the time ! That pair's never out of their beds yet ! I'll need to go and waken them up myself !' She opened the kitchen door and called piercingly, 'Peter ! Maisie ! Are you never up yet ? You'll be late for your work !'

'Aw,' sighed Willie, 'can ye no' think o' somethin' different tae say by's "Ye'll be late fur yer work"? It wid dae mair guid if ye wis tae cry "Hurry up ! It's ham an' Aiberdeen haddy an' twa eggs fur yer breakfast."'

'Ah-you !' They jostled against each other in the tiny scullery. 'Here, let me into the sink.'

'Jeengs, Serah, ye're ower sonsy tae get intae that wee jaw-box nooadays.'

'None of your nonsense !' She filled the kettle, which had had only a spoonful of water in it, and withdrew from the tap, saying, 'You get washed now—and hurry up, or——'

'Ah'll be late fur ma work,' he agreed affably.

Just then the door burst open and Peter and Maisie poured in half dressed.

'Hullo, Mother—you're up !' exclaimed Peter.

'Is this another of Dad's little jokes ? Or did I dream that he said he was going for the doctor ?' demanded Maisie.

'So Ah wis goin' fur the doctor !' Willie delayed his ablutions to justify himself. 'Yer mother went aff 'er heid fur a while there.'

'Are you all right now, Mother ?' asked Peter tenderly.

'I'm fine, son. I just thought I'd like to have a day in bed, but I couldn't bear it.'

'Couldn't bear what ?' asked Maisie. 'To lie still ?'

'No. Never mind. You hurry up. It's a quarter-past seven. You'll be late for your work.'

'Good heavens!' exclaimed Peter, and in a moment the two young folk had scuttled away. The significant sound of the bathroom door's being snibbed sent Willie into a torrent of rage:

'Is that Peter away intae the bathroom afore me? Ah'll set fire tae's shirt tail!'

'Willie! Don't be vulgar!' said Sarah. 'See here—you can wash yourself at the sink.'

'But Peter knows fine Ah'm first fur the bathroom in the mornin'. An' onywey, hoo can Ah wash masel' in this jawbox? It's bung-fu' o' pots an' tea-leafs!'

'Don't exaggerate!' ordered Sarah, lifting out the solitary small pot and sluicing away the half-dozen tea-leaves.

'Whit aboot a towel?' He held up a damp rag that was hanging on a nail behind the door. 'Will Ah use this?'

'No, stupid! That's the cloth for washing the stairs! See, there's a clean towel on the roller there!'

'Whit soap am Ah tae use?' he continued, contemplating the choice of a cake of scrubbing-soap, a piece of pumice-stone, and a potato-peeler.

Sarah poked him with the scrubbing-soap. 'Here you are! Do you want me to wash you—you big baby?'

'Ach, lea'e me alane! Away an' tell Peter tae hurry up oota that bathroom.'

'I'll do nothing of the kind. I can hear Maisie yelling on him to let her in.'

'The cheek o' hur!' Willie stopped lathering his hands to express himself on the subject of filial disrespect. He concluded only when he had resumed and finished washing his face. After that he reverted to type, and demanded to know where his wife had planked the towel he had laid in full view.

'It's at your side on the sink there!'

'Pit it intae ma hauns, well. Ma eyes is fu' o' soap.'

Performing the duties of a personal maid, Sarah put the towel into his hands saying, 'For goodness' sake hurry up, Willie. You'll be late for your work. Look at the time!'

Just then Maisie ran in excitedly. 'Mother, for heaven's sake tell Peter to get out of the bathroom. If it's that time already——'

'Oh, give him a chance, Maisie. He'll be shaving.'

'Shaving! Huh, all *he's* got could come off with an india-rubber. He's been in there for *hours*.' She rushed away again, shouting, 'Peter, you sneak! You're just trying to make me late for school!'

Above the rattling of the handle of the bathroom door Willie's voice could be heard: 'Heh, Maisie, don't you go in tae that bathroom afore me!'

Back came the retort, 'I'll jolly well go in before you if I like!'

'Here—that's no' the wey tae talk tae yer faither! Ah've a guid mind tae——'

'Oh, go and play peever! . . . Peter! You brute!' Once again the handle rattled.

'Wid ye listen tae that, Serah,' complained Willie drying himself with a deal of puffing and blowing. 'She jist talks tae me as if Ah wis one o' the weans in 'er class at the school.'

'Oh, stop worrying about that, Willie. You get ahead.'

'Are ye makin' up ma piece?'

'Yes.'

'Whit's in it?'

'Spam.'

'Ach—Spam again!'

'I thought you liked it.'

'So Ah did, but efter the first hunner times the novelty kinna wears aff. Whit aboot a coupla hard-b'iled eggs?'

'I haven't an egg in the house.'

Maisie's voice reached them again from the region of the bathroom-door. 'Oh, Peter, hurry! You've been in there long enough to shave the towels as well.'

'Don't be so impatient, Maisie,' implored her mother, joining the girl at her post in the lobby. 'Peter, son,' shouted Sarah through the bathroom-door. 'You'll be late for your work! It's half-past seven!'

Maisie rattled the door handle once more, insisting, 'Peter, you *must* let me in !'

'Away an' bile yer can, Maisie !' exclaimed Willie, also appearing on the spot. 'It's me next !'

'You should've been up earlier and got in before this,' was Maisie's unjust retort.

'Nane o' yer lip ! Ah wis up afore you onywey. When Ah wis your age——'

'Yes,' sneered the girl, 'you were putting out stair-lights in your bare feet for sixpence a week. We've heard it all before ! *Peter !*'

From the other side of the bathroom-door came a gargle of disgust. 'I've cut myself !'

'My-my !' mocked his father. 'He's cut 'issel' ! Send fur Geordie Geddes !' Then in a burst of rage, 'Will you come oota there !'

Sarah tried to soothe her husband : 'Willie, don't be angry with him if he's cut himself. Peter, son, come on out and I'll sort it for you !'

'Huh, Mummy's darling !' observed Maisie as the door opened. 'Here he comes ! He should have used an india-rubber like I said. Peter, my infant, you're too young to be trusted with a razor.'

'I'll remember that the next time you ask me to shave the back of your neck !' threatened Peter.

'Don't worry ! That style went out years ago !' Maisie got so interested in her self-justification that she took her eye off the bathroom-door for a moment and her father slipped in, banging the door in triumph behind him. Once again she shook the door by the handle. 'Dad ! You beast ! It was *my* turn !'

Sarah laid a persuasive hand on the girl's arm : 'Come on and get your breakfast while you're waiting, Maisie. The porridge is just on the boil.'

'Oh, stop trying to boss me !'

'What makes you so carnaptious in the mornings ?' demanded Sarah as the three of them made for the kitchen. 'I'm sure you don't need to carry on like that !'

' She's turning into a girny old maid ! ' suggested Peter.

' You shut your trap ! '

' Peter,' said Sarah, ' would you like me to get you some sticking-plaster for that cut on your face ? '

' Ugh, it's okay,' replied Peter, feeling manly.

Said Maisie, ' After all that fuss I expected we'd have to call an ambulance.'

Before Peter could retort, or they had any of them reached the kitchen, they were caught up sharply by a howl from the bathroom. The door opened, and Willie advanced holding something in his hand : ' Look whit Ah've went an' done ! Broke ma fause teeth ! ' His speech was even more inarticulate than usual.

' That,' declared Maisie, ' is what you get for barging into the bathroom out of your turn.' Determined not to be caught a second time, she seized the opportunity of slipping into the bathroom, an action that called forth another howl from her father.

' Heh, Maisie ! Ah'm no' feenished in there ! Ah've tae dae ma hair yet ! ' Realizing the futility of going on shouting, he turned to his wife, ' Serah—look at ma teeth. In twa bits ! '

' You'll have to live on saps now, Dad,' interposed Peter.

' Oh dear, isn't that terrible, and the McLeathers coming for tea to-night. You look so fushionless without your teeth. My ! you're a careless lump, so you are, Willie.'

' Ah didnae *try* tae dae it.'

Peter pulled at his mother's dressing-gown. ' Here, come on with the breakfast, Mother.'

Once again the procession moved in the direction of the kitchen, this time with more success. In a moment or two both men were seated at the table.

' Anything to follow the porridge ? ' asked Peter.

' Yes, a wee bit ham and potato scone fried.'

' Good enough ! '

' Ach, hoo can Ah eat ham wantin' ma teeth ? ' grumbled Willie.

' You could dip it in your tea and sook ! ' suggested his son.

'Ach you!'

Maisie chose that moment to flounce into the kitchen, snapping, 'Peter, you skunk! You've used up all my toothpaste!'

'I never touched it!' he stormed.

'You must have. The tube's empty!'

'Go on! Tell me I'm a liar!'

'Peter!' exclaimed his mother. 'Don't be vulgar!'

'That's not being vulgar! That's only——'

'Shut up, everybody!' mouthed Willie gummily. 'It wis me, Maisie. Ah musta used ower much, fur ma teeth skited oota ma hauns intae the handbasin. Jeengs, hoo'm Ah gonnae get on wantin' them?'

'Serve you jolly well right!' tossed back Maisie. 'I hope your rabbits die!'

'Whit rabbits? Ah havenae got ony!'

'Oh, forget it!' She bounced out of the kitchen again.

'Maisie!' called Sarah after her. 'Don't rush away like that. Sit down and take your breakfast.'

'I'll sit down when it suits me!' The bathroom-door was banged on the words.

'What a way to talk to me!' wailed Sarah. 'I wonder what's the matter with her these days?'

'She's been like that in the mornings since ever I knew her!' observed Peter.

At that, an idea struck Willie: 'Here—Ah tell ye whit, Serah. Whaur's yon auld set o' teeth Ah had?'

'You told me to throw them out.'

'Ah never done ony sich thing!'

'You did so! I gave them away!'

'Ye whit! Who did ye gi'e them tae? Somebody we know?'

'I gave them to a woman at the door. She gave me ninepence for them.'

'Ninepence! Ninepence! No' even a fern in a pot forbye? Ye michta known Ah widda needed them again.'

'You told me——'

'Ach you! Ye're aye sellin' things at the door!'

'The correct quotation, Dad,' pointed out Peter, 'is "Ye're aye tyin' yer shoe-lace."'

'Ah never said a word aboot ma shoe-lace!'

The lad decided to drop the argument. 'I'll take my ham now, Mother,' he said. 'And Dad's lot too, seeing he won't be able to eat his.'

'Ye will nut!' blazed Willie.

'Eh will sut!' returned Peter politely but firmly.

'Peter!' put in Sarah, 'don't talk like that to your father! Willie—I'll make you an omelette with some dried egg.'

'Away wi' ye! Ah hivnae time tae wait fur that. Jeengs, this is a scunner, so it is! Ah wonder if the dentist could mend ma teeth while Ah'm waitin'?'

'Can't you stick the bits together with the gum in your mouth?' asked Peter with adolescent glee at his own wit.

'Wait you, ma lad, tae ye've tae wear fause teeth yersel'. Ye'll no' be sae perky. Heh, Serah, whit am Ah tae dae aboot ma teeth?'

'Oh,' resignedly, 'I suppose I'd better take them to the dentist for you.'

'Well,' declared the man with the air of a martyr, 'it's yer ain fau't—pittin' the wind up me this mornin' wi' yer palavers aboot lying in bed. Peter—see's ower some mair mulk.'

'There's not much left.'

'There never is, efter you've had yer whack at it.'

'D'you want toast, Willie?' asked Sarah.

'Naw—toast wid jag ma gums.'

The door opened once more, and Maisie announced that anybody who wished could have the use of the bathroom now.

'How gracious of you!' acknowledged her brother with some sarcasm.

Ignoring the comment, Maisie asked if the post had arrived.

'No,' answered her mother. 'And neither has the milk. I've never known it to be so late before. Sit down, Maisie, your porridge will be getting cold.'

'Ugh!' exclaimed the girl, peering into the depths of the milk jug on the table. 'Yesterday's milk! Looks curdled to me. I'm not wanting any porridge.'

Speaking with his mouth full, her father said, 'We'd need tae keep a pig in this hoose tae eat up your scraps, Maisie.'

'We've only got to watch you eating, Dad, to know that we *are* keeping a pig!'

'Maisie!' stormed Sarah, 'don't you *dare* to talk to your father like that!'

'H'm! I've heard you say worse than that to him yourself —many a time!'

'That's different. Here's your ham. I expect there'll be something wrong with it next.'

'I'll eat it for you,' offered Peter, whose stomach, in his mother's opinion, was like a bottomless pit. 'It's terribly salt, you know.'

'I'll taste it first. The potato scone looks frazzled, Mother. You know I don't like it overdone!'

'Well,' snapped Sarah, 'you should get up earlier and cook it for yourself! I wish I *had* stayed in my bed. You're an ungrateful lot, so you are!'

'I never said a word!' Peter was indignant.

'Don't argue! You've no time!'

'Ugh, I can't eat this!' said Maisie. 'The ham's frazzled too. Lassie! Lassie! Come and get something to eat.'

'Maisie!' protested Sarah, 'You're not to give the dog good ham! See, give it to me! I'll put it into the soup!'

Maisie handed over her plate, with the query, 'Has the paper come?'

'Naw,' said her father. 'Everythin's behind this mornin'— like the coo's tail.'

'Oh, Willie,' wailed his wife, 'don't bother your head about such things as cows' tails. Look at the time—you'll be late for your work.'

'Mother!' the exclamation came from Peter. 'Every morning in life except Sundays you tell us to "look at the time, you'll be late for your work." But do we look at the time?' he asked oratorically. ' No ! Why ? It's a case of the constant dropping that wears away the stone.'

' In your case, my pet,' put in Maisie, ' it's much more like the truth that you're too confoundedly scared somebody pinches something off your plate to turn round and look at the clock.'

' And in your case, my precious, you're too bloomin' lazy to move your ba——'

' Peter ! ' shouted Sarah hurriedly. ' Don't be vulgar ! Look at the——'

' I know,' said Peter calmly. ' " Look at the time, you'll be late for your work ! " '

' Here ! ' Willie blurted out in consternation, ' whit time did ye say it wis, Serah ? '

' Twenty-five to eight,' she replied.

' Whaur did ye see that ? '

' The alarm—on the mantelpiece ! '

' Huh—look at the big clock on the wa',' and he pointed derisively.

She looked, and so peculiar was her manner that the other two looked also. ' Twenty-five past six ! ' they all exclaimed.

' Mother ! ' demanded Peter, ' are you playing a game ? '

' I am not ! What on earth has happened ? I knew the alarm was ten minutes fast, of course.'

' Ah'll tell ye whit's happened ! ' Willie's face was wrinkled with amusement although his smile was toothless. ' Ah pit back the big clock on the wa' on Saturday night for the changin' o' the hour fur Summer Time, but Ah never touched the alarm. An' we never use the alarm on Sunday mornin's.'

Peter got up, stretched himself and said, ' Twenty-five past six ! I'm away back to my bed. See and have another breakfast ready for me in an hour, Mother.' He went out quickly.

Maisie's reaction was different. Her sleepy crossness seemed to have vanished. ' Well, folks,' she said quite amiably, ' it's a glorious morning ! I think I'll walk to school.'

As for Willie, he sucked his lips and said, ' Help ma boab—a' that rush fur nothin'. An' me wi' a set o' broken fause teeth forbye ! Ach—weemin ! '

CHAPTER 8

WHERE THERE'S A WILL THERE'S A FRAY

THERE are occasions in the lives of the best of us when we fail to show up to our best advantage. Such an occasion arose in Sarah's life the following Saturday afternoon. The postman had rattled the letterbox in such a way that Maisie, always hopeful for some correspondence for herself, rushed to the door. She came back into the kitchen with slow steps and a world of wonder in her voice as she said :

' It's for you, Dad. A letter, no less ! '

' Fur me ? Who f'ae ? '

' How should I know ? ' she demanded, handing over the communication.

Peter's suggestion was that it would begin, ' Dear Sir, Unless you pay me within three days——'

Sarah's was, ' Don't sit gaping at it, Willie. The postmark won't help you. Open it.'

But the postmark completely puzzled Willie. He said it looked like Argyllshire, and that he knew nobody in that part of the world.

' Well, send it back,' said Peter.

' Here—let me open it ! ' Sarah stretched out her hand.

' Naw, ye'll no' ! ' With an effort of courage, Willie shoved his thumb into the flap and tore open the envelope, saying, ' This micht be f'ae ma rich uncle in Australia.' He read, haltingly, ' " Mr. Wm. McFlannel, Dear Sir, So I—expert—ing—none address will coming—nothing to for——" ' He gave up the attempt to make sense out of the writing, exclaiming, ' Aw Jeengs ! Did ye ever see sichna hand-o'-write ! '

' Here, let me see it ! ' ordered Peter. In a moment he had announced that the missive came from Achnaclachan.

' Achnaclachan ! ' repeated Maisie. ' Sounds like outside sanitation.'

'Maisie!' Sarah's reaction was typical. 'Don't be vulgar!'

Peter proceeded to read the letter. '"Mr. Wm. McFlannel, Dear Sir, As I expect my name and address will convey nothing to you, perhaps I had better explain that I am the minister of this parish——"'

'Help ma boab!' cried Willie in amazement, 'imagine a meenister writin' tae me!'

'"I am sorry to have to tell you that your aged aunt—Miss Jeanie McFlannel—died here suddenly a few hours ago."'

'Auld Auntie!' gasped Willie. 'Ah mind noo she went tae some place at the backa beyond when the war broke oot.'

There was very little grief in Sarah's voice as she put in, 'I know what it is! She's needing the money to bury her— the mean old bizzum!'

'Wheesht, Serah!' ordered the bereaved nephew. 'Cairry on, Peter.'

'"As you probably know, she came here as an evacuee and has dwelt in our midst——"' Peter looked at his sister with the remark that that was a right sanctimonious phrase if ever there was one, Maisie agreeing with the additional comment that he sounded as if he spoke with a holy whine.

'Hey, cut the cackle an' get on wi't!' said Willie.

'". . . has dwelt in our midst until the time of her call. Consequently there is no-one apart from myself to look after her affairs, and I have just found among her papers a Will in which she appoints you her sole executor."'

'What!' cried Sarah. 'The impiddence of her!'

'You haud yer tongue. Go on, Peter!'

'"I should be glad therefore if you could come here, as soon as possible, and take over the final funeral arrangements. Yours faithfully, R. M'Cassock."'

'Well, I never!' gasped Sarah.

Willie, however, was giving reign to the sentimental urge within him. 'Puir Auld Auntie! Imagine hur passin' away 'er lief alane.'

'Well, she only had herself to blame for that!' said Sarah with some spirit. 'She was a bad-tempered, cantankerous, nasty-minded old woman, and if it wasn't that I never speak ill of the dead, I could say a few things about her. It'll cost you a bonny penny to go to that place—what's it called ? '

'Achnaclachan.' Peter supplied the information after exchanging a meaning look with Maisie, who said :

'I say, Dad—she wouldn't have left a Will if she'd had nothing to leave——'

Peter took up the theme. 'And Dad's sole executor ! '

'Eh ? ' gulped Willie. 'Whit's that ye're sayin' ? '

Before the young folk could repeat themselves, Sarah made a solemn declaration to the effect that she would not put on a stitch of mourning for the departed lady, but Peter was equally determined to find out about the financial standing of the deceased.

'Dad ! ' he urged. 'Waken up ! Did Old Auntie have any money ? '

'Eh ? '

'Money, Dad. Bawbees. Sillar. Did Old Auntie have any ? ' Maisie prodded him with an exasperated finger.

'Ah—Ah don't— Oh, Ah mind noo ! She got willed a whit-ye-may-ca'-it f'ae an auld lady she wis servant tae when she wis a lassie. Fifty pound a year it wis.'

'What ! ' blurted out Sarah. 'The two-faced old heathen—going about the way she did—scrounging for all she could get.'

Willie ignored the observation. He went on meditatively, 'An' she kep' a wee shop fur years—och, she'll be gey weel gaithered ! '

'See here, Dad,' said Peter, 'how old would she be when she got this annuity ? '

'Wait tae Ah think. Aboot twenty-five, say.'

'And how old is she now ? I mean——'

'Och, she'll be seeventy-five if she's a day.'

'Aha ! ' exclaimed Maisie. 'Fifty pounds for fifty years—two thousand five hundred pounds ! '

'What ! ' This time Sarah's astonishment compelled her to sit down clutching her throat. 'Two thousand ! What are you talking about ? Willie—why did you never tell me this before ? '

'Ach, it never entered ma heid tae tell ye. Ah thocht ye knew. An' onywey, ye never liked 'er.'

'And you're sole executor, Dad,' Maisie pointed out.

'Whit? Me? Ach, there must be some mistake.'

Slowly the implication dawned on Sarah. She was quite overcome by emotion as she reached out a hand to her husband, saying, 'Oh, Willie! All that money! Oh dear-dear! I had no idea!'

'Good old Dad!' cried Maisie, thumping the sole executor on the back. 'Congratulations!'

Peter joined in the thumping process with the comment, 'You deserve it, Dad!'

All of which convinced Willie that, for some reason or other he had fallen heir to some property, but he had the modesty to insist that he was not aware of having done anything to merit such good fortune.

Said Maisie, 'Maybe we'll be able to flit to a decent locality now. Bearsden or——'

At that Willie came to life thoroughly. 'Here, shut up, you! Let me think. Ah've tae go tae the funeral. Ah wonder if Ah should let oor Mattha know. An' Geordie——'

'You'll do nothing of the kind,' said Sarah. 'You'd have to pay their fares for one thing. And anyway they've never had the slightest interest in their old aunt.' There was a complete reversal of her own attitude towards the dead woman, but she seemed oblivious of the fact as she went on, 'See—I'll need to look out your black suit. And what about me? I'd be better to go, too, wouldn't I?'

'Naw, ye'll no' bother yersel',' said Willie brutally. 'Ye've changed yer tune in an awful hurry. Here—see's me a *Murray's Diary* tae Ah fin' oot aboot trains tae that Achnaplace.'

'Oh dear-dear!' whimpered Sarah, getting to her feet and preparing to speed her husband on his melancholy journey. 'Two thousand five hundred pounds! I wish I hadn't used all my clothing coupons.'

'Whatever for, Mother?' asked Maisie.

'Well, the least we can do is to show some sort of respect to the poor old soul!' She left the kitchen with the promise to look out Willie's 'things.'

For a few minutes there was silence in the kitchen. Willie was busy with the advertisements in the *Murray's Diary*, while Maisie and Peter allowed their thoughts to roam unhindered in the realms of airy castles. After a bit Maisie suggested they ought to send a notice to the papers.

'Yes!' Peter was full of enthusiasm. 'And what about a wee poem?'

'The very ham-and-haddy!' returned Maisie. 'Wait till I think——'

At that Sarah came back complaining that the only white shirt she could find was very yellow looking.

'Ach, Ah'll jist wear ma dickey!' decided Willie.

'You'll do nothing of the kind!' was Sarah's retort. 'And her leaving you three thousand pounds!'

'*Two* thousan'—an' maybe she's spent it a'.'

'Not her! She was too mean to spend a ha'penny on a car fare! To think of her having all that money and scrounging the way she did——'

Willie raised his eyes from the railway time-table. 'Here— you get on wi' lookin' oot ma claes fur the funeral. Maybe ma black suit'll no' fit me.'

As Sarah disappeared once more for those regions below the various beds where she stowed away seldom-used garments Peter shouted:

'I've got it, Maisie. Listen:

> Oor Auntie Jeanie
> Had pains in 'er peenie,
> She took to her bed,
> And—ehm longed to be dead.'

'That's rubbish,' said his sister with scorn. 'You'd be better with an honest-to-goodness McGonagle. Something about "Oh wonderful Auntie McFlannel."' She pondered the point for a moment or two, then came away with:

> 'Oh wonderful Auntie McFlannel,
> She kep' a' 'er sillar in a joog wantin' a han'le.'

93

'Pf! That's worse!' was Peter's response. 'What about something for her tombstone?'

'Huh! "Beneath this sod lies another."'

'Oh, let's have something original,' pleaded Peter, as his mother returned to the kitchen.

Once again Willie laid aside the study of the lilac-covered booklet. 'Ah'm jist thinkin', Serah, wid ma navy blue suit an' ma bowler hat no' be guid anuff?'

'What! And you getting all that money? You're dressing yourself in your best, my man!'

'But *she'll* no' see me!'

'Don't be irreverent. And anyway, it's a shame you having this lovely suit and you hardly ever get the chance to wear it.'

'Ah'm savin' it up fur Maisie's weddin'.'

'Huh!' snorted Peter, 'it'll be out the fashion and in again before Maisie's taken off the shelf. Jeanie—meanie—Sheenie—cheeny——'

Not fully alive to the significance of her son's poetic meanderings, Sarah asked Willie how long he thought he would be away from home.

'Hoo should Ah know? Ah've never been a sole executioner in ma life afore.'

To which understatement Sarah paid no attention, merely remarking that he would need black socks.

'Ach, don't fuss! Ma boots'll hide ma socks.'

'Willie, don't be so callous! You *must* wear black socks—anything less wouldn't be respectful and her leaving you all that money. Ehm . . .' A calculating look came into her eye. 'I'm just thinking, Willie . . .'

Willie seemed suddenly absorbed in the search for Achnaclachan in the time-table, while Maisie murmured a mournful, experimental dirge, 'McFlannel . . . han'le . . . panel . . . can'le . . .' Sarah, however, continued undaunted:

'About mournings, Willie. A black fox fur would be very nice.'

'Ah'm no' needin' nae black fox fur!' he declared.

94

'Ugh, you ! I mean a black fox fur for me ! Mrs. M'Cotton's got one. . . .'

While she waited for a reply, Maisie's murmur continued, ' Here *lies* all that's *left* of old *Auntie McFlannel*,' but her mother was too intent on her own purposes. She went on :

' Willie—you're not listening ! I said Mrs. M'Cotton's got a new black fox fur——'

' Ach, Serah, don't bother me the noo an' me lookin' up trains.'

' That's right—change the subject. Just as soon as I try to get something for myself ! You're mean, so you are, and you with all that money ! '

But once again Willie seemed determined to talk about something else. ' Heh ! ' he exclaimed, ' whit the bleezes are ye pittin' oot that semmit an' things fur ? Ye surely don't expec' me tae shift tae the buff an' it no' ma bath night ! '

' It's the least you can do for the poor old soul ! ' insisted Sarah.

' Auntie . . . cantie . . . pantie . . .' murmured Peter.

' Here *lies* all that's *left* of old . . .' jingled Maisie.

' I feel heart-sorry for the poor old soul,' continued Sarah mournfully, ' ending her days in that lonely wee place without any of her own kith and kin to close her eyes for her.'

' Heh, screw aff the waterworks, Serah,' advised Willie.

' Are you sure you wouldn't like me to come with you ? After all, you're her sole ex——'

' Ah'm goin' masel' ! ' declared Willie firmly. ' Ye can send a wreath if ye like.'

' I will that — the best that money can buy. I only wish,' she sniffed, ' that I'd been kinder to her when she was alive.'

' Help ma boab ! ' exclaimed the astonished heir-apparent, ' you're the one fur changin' yer mind.'

At that Maisie thumped the table : ' I've got it !

Here *lies* all that's *left* of Old *Auntie McFlannel*,
She *gave* up the *ghost* while a-*swim*-ming the *channel*.'

95

'No,' said Peter with sweeping condemnation. 'I tell you what!

'Here lies all that's left of Old Auntie McFlannel,
     Her whiskers caught fire when she was snuffin' the can'le.'

Their mother interrupted their laughter with, 'What are you two giggling at? Have you no respect for the dead?'

Willie, however, refused to allow her activities to be side-tracked. 'Heh,' he ejaculated, 'that's no' a flee-away collar ye've laid oot fur me!'

'Of course! It's the right thing to wear with a morning suit.'

'But Ah'm no' gonnae be singin' at nae socials! An' fur ony favour, be sure an' pack ma navy suit. Ah'm no' goin' aboot the streets of Achna-clachna-thingummy lookin' like as if Ah'd lost ma cab! Here—see's me ma lum hat tae Ah try it on.'

Sarah handed over the headgear, with the injunction to watch not to ruffle the pile. Willie smoothed the sides of the hat with his cuff, set it on his head at a jaunty angle, and, peering at his reflection in the mirror above the mantelpiece, demanded of the family that they look at him. 'Mphm!' said he with intense self-satisfaction. 'No' bad—eh, Maisie?'

'You'd look a fat sight better,' said she coldly, 'if you weren't in your shirt-sleeves.'

'Ach, you!' Turning to his wife, he asked her if she didn't think he was looking remarkably fit for a man of his years, adding, 'Heh, Serah, if Ah wis a younger man wid ye mairry me again?'

But Sarah had scoffed at that suggestion too often in the past to be thrilled with it now. 'Don't be so irreverent!' she retorted, 'and poor Old Auntie lying——'

'Ach, take ma hat, somebody,' pleaded Willie with great disgust at his wife's continued assumption of grief, 'before Ah take the bo——'

'Willie!' shouted Sarah just in time.

'Well, ye fair scunner me goin' on like that. Here, Peter,' he added, tossing the railway time-table over to his son, 'see if ye can find that Achna- place fur me.'

The versifying contest being thus rudely brought to an end, the next hour became a repeat performance of the pantomime that took place every night Willie went on Home Guard duty, so we shall leave the family to get on with their own private storm in a teacup and return to their midst a week later.

The kitchen was full to overflowing with all the ramifications of the McFlannel clan. Willie's brother George and Mrs. George were there, as were also Mattha-of-the-adenoidal speech and his wife Biddy ; their sister Jeanie, now Mrs. McTape, was also in attendance, together with aunts and uncles and cousins unto the third and fourth generation, all of them clamouring for self-expression. Mrs. George, by reason of the stridulatory quality of her voice, gained the company's attention by shrieking :

'Whit Ah say is—whit kinna-like wey wis that fur tae let the relatives know auld Auntie wis deid—an advert*ise*ment in the papers ?'

'Ay,' agreed her sister-in-law Mrs. McTape, 'an' some o' us never even seen hit ! '

'Imagine that ! ' mourned Mattha.

'It wis a fair disgrace ! ' declared Geordie, 'so it wis ! Ah jist said tae the wife here—" Oor Wullie's gonnae get a piece o' ma mind ! " '

Sarah, in the vortex of the maelstrom, flapped her hands helplessly. 'Good gracious,' she retorted, her voice shrill with excitement and anger, 'how were we to know you were all so anxious about Old Auntie ? Some of you haven't clapped eyes on her for manys a long day.'

'Clapped eyes on 'er ! ' tossed back Mrs. Geordie. 'Ah like that ! An' us got the len' o' a coupla quid affa 'er jist last year.'

Her husband, however, taking a very poor view of this revelation, requested her to shut up and not give the show away, but the finer points of the scene between husband and wife were missed altogether by Mrs. McTape, who exclaimed oratorically :

'Whit Ah want tae know is—hoo oor Wullie managed tae

worm 'issel' intae gettin' 'er tae leave him a' 'er money—an' me wis cried Jeanie efter 'er !'

'That's right,' agreed her brother Mattha, 'an' five thousand pound, tae !'

'*Four* thousand !' corrected Sarah.

'It's a lie !' The denunciation came from Geordie. 'It's five thousand if it's a penny, an' the wife an' me is mair entitled tae it than onybody else. Efter a' we done fur the auld wumman.'

This statement laid the author open to an attack from his own sister. 'Whit did *youse* ever dae fur 'er ?' she demanded.

Flinging herself into the whirlpool to the rescue of her husband, Mrs. Geordie stated, 'Manys a time she dropped intae oor hoose fur a cuppy tea.'

'Huh—gey wersh tea it wid be, Ah'll bet,' observed her sister-in-law. 'The slops het up, likely.'

'Here you !' threatened Mrs. Geordie, 'Ah'll bash ye if ye say a thing like that again.'

Surprisingly, Mattha's voice made itself heard above the ensuing din. 'Ay, but here—whit aboot me ? Ah yince mended 'er auld nock fur 'er.'

'Huh,' sneered his brother, 'hoo much did she hiv tae pey ye fur daein' it, but ?'

Once again Sarah flapped her hands : 'Listen, everybody—if you'll all be quiet, I'll read you the letter I got from Willie this morning.'

'It's no' 'is letter we're wantin' tae hear,' declared the letter-writer's sister, 'it's 'imsel'. Wait tae Ah get the haud o' 'im ! Five thousand pound, an' ma weans withoot a stitch tae their backs.'

'Well, who's fau't is that ?' inquired Mrs. Geordie. 'If ye werenae sichna thowless bizzum ye'd look efter yer weans better.'

At that Mrs. McTape rose to vindicate her honour. 'Heh, get oota ma road, Mattha,' she roared, ''till Ah clout 'er jaw fur sayin' that tae me.'

As Peter sprang forward to separate the contestants, the door-bell rang. Maisie, going to the door, pointed out that the kitchen would not hold any more people, yet in a moment or two she was announcing the arrival of Mr. and Mrs. James McFlannelette. Instantly the quarrel between Mrs. George McFlannel and Mrs. Jeanie McTape was forgotten ; united, they turned on the new-comers and exclaimed, one after the other :

' Well, if they're comin' in, Ah'm goin' oot ! ' and ' Ah'm no' gonnae stey here in the same hoose wi' sichna coupla twisters ! '

The pandemonium that followed wracked Sarah's genteel soul ; mindful of her equally genteel neighbours, she yearned after some device wherewith to quell the riot. She cleared her throat.

' Peter ! ' she screamed above the din, ' away and ask the woman next door for some more chairs.'

' She said she hadn't any left the last time,' roared Peter in reply.

Maisie's comment that no-one was as yet sitting on the bunker was drowned in the rising flood of family affection.

' Well,' shouted Sarah, ' get the police, Peter.'

The effect was instantaneous in its silence ; a peeved voice demanded, ' Whit aboot that letter f'ae Wullie, then ? '

' Well, for goodness' sake keep quiet, everybody,' said Sarah fumbling with an envelope, ' this is a respectable neighbourhood —not the slums like what some of you seem to come from.'

' Who's fau't's that, well ? ' demanded Mrs. George. ' If we had wur rights——'

' Shut up, you ! ' commanded her lord and master. ' Let's wait tae we hear whit Wullie's got tae say.'

In a rather restless stillness, Sarah read aloud : ' " Dear Sarah, I hope this finds you as well as it leaves me. You will be surprised to hear that Old Auntie left over four thousand pounds. . . . " '

' Imagine that ! ' interpolated Mattha, while his brother in-sisted all over again that the amount was five thousand—a remark that threatened to let loose the dogs of war. Sarah, irritated by the uproar, forgot herself so far as to drop into the vernacular as she yelled, ' Peter—away for the polis ! ' It was a language, however, that was fully understood by her uninvited guests, and they responded as she had hoped they would. The dogs of war retired, growling, to their kennels, keeping watch while the reading of the letter was renewed :

' "I managed to get the lawyers to put things through quick for me, so I'll be home on Saturday with the train that gets in at 7 o'clock. Your loving husband, W. McFlannel. P.S.—See and have a good feed ready for me." '

The postscript called forth the comment from Mrs. George, ' The callous brute—aye the same—nothin' in 'is heid but 'is stummick ! '

To which Mrs. McTape added, ' Nae wunner he wants a guid feed efter stealin' a' that money affa 'is ain flesh an' blood.'

' He didn't steal it ! ' shrieked Sarah hysterically. ' Oh dear, I wish he'd come. He should be here any minute now.'

' Won't he be delighted to see such a happy family gathering to welcome him ? ' said Maisie, not without some sneering in both her voice and her manner.

' Whit's up wi' you, ma lady,' pointed out her Uncle George, ' is that ye've aye been too big fur yer boots ! ' while his wife added :

' Ach, theym school teachers is a' the same.'

Maisie's Aunt Jeanie contributed, ' Ay, an' wi' a' this money she's got by jookery-pokery, there'll be nae haudin' 'er in ! '

This statement was received with such enthusiasm by the visitors that an impartial observer might have been excused for jumping to the conclusion that a free fight was in progress. No blame, therefore, is attached to Willie for coming in at that moment, shouting :

' Heh-heh, whit's goin' on here ? Is this a private row or can onybody jine in ? '

In a moment Sarah was sobbing on her husband's breast in a silence that was caused partly by surprise and partly by embarrassment. The expression on the faces of the company made Willie say :

' Whit are ye a' sittin' there wi' faces like torn melodeons fur ? '

' They're jealous, Willie—that's what it is ! ' declared Sarah from her safe refuge.

' We're no' jealous,' said Mattha. ' We're jist up fur tae see that we get wur rights.'

' Ay ! ' Willie's brothers were united in purpose for once in their lives, for it was Geordie who was saying, ' We want fur tae see justice done ! '

Then Mrs. Geordie joined in : ' Efter a' Ah done fur Auld Auntie—tae think she never even left me as much as a tin teapot.'

This remark was not very well received by some of the back-benchers, but, no doubt feeling that their claims were of secondary importance, they held their peace while Willie eased himself of the burden of his wife, his hat and his suitcase. Peter, taking charge of the last mentioned, urged his father to cheer up, he had never died a winter yet. Willie ignored the advice, exclaiming :

' If somebody wid gie me a sate——"

' Oh, get'm a diamond-studded throne ! ' sneered Mrs. McTape.

Sarah drew forward the chair on which she herself had been sitting : ' Here you are, Willie. Ehm—was everything all right ? '

' Ay. Oh ay ! ' he assured her, sitting down and deliberately misunderstanding her question. ' She's lyin' in a bonnie wee kirkyaird up on the hillside.'

' That's very nice, but what about—I mean—— ' Sarah was reluctant to be frank in the presence of her enemies.

' Oh, the funeral ? ' Willie continued his deploying campaign. ' Oh, it wis a gey quiet affair—jist the meenister an' twa-three neeburs an' me.'

' Yes-yes, but what about the other thing—you know—— '

' Ye mean the funeral tea ? Och, it wasnae jist exactly as guid as a pre-war tightener wi' steak pie an' a' that, but we managed tae get plenty bully beef.'

' Willie ! ' Sarah's exasperation, coming on top of her previous distraction, was making her lose her affectionate demeanour towards her husband. ' You know quite well what I mean.'

Mattha came to her rescue. ' Withoot ony mair beatin' aboot the bush, Wullie, jist hoo much money did Auld Auntie leave ? '

' Oh that ? ' Willie's manner was engagingly off-hand. ' It wis—let me see—— ' He fished in an inner pocket. ' Ah've got a note o't somewhere. Ay. Here we are——' A document was unfolded in a hush of expectancy. 'Four thousand one hundred and thirty-one pounds.'

The amount was repeated by everyone in the room except Peter and Maisie, who kept in the background so as to enjoy the performance to the full. Their Aunt Jeanie was the first to make an individual expression of opinion :

'Whit Ah want tae know is—whit kinna swindlin's been goin' on that she left it a' tae you ! Whit aboot ma puir wee weans ?'

The claim of her offspring, however, was not deemed to be justified by the rest of the company, for the clamour that broke out in protest caused Willie to shout :

'Shut up ! Heh—SHUT UP ! Ye'll hae the neeburs hammerin' on us. Listen tae me, folks. SHE DIDNAE LEAVE IT A' TAE ME !'

Even Peter was astounded by this piece of information, for he asked, 'Were you not sole executor after all, Dad ?'

'Ay—sole executor, but that's different f'ae bein' sole whit-ye-may-ca'-it—legatee. Here—Ah've got the will in ma pooch. You read it oot, Peter.'

There was no need to call for silence as the young fellow unfolded the stiff paper, Maisie leaning over his shoulder as he read :

' " I, Jean McFlannel, Spinster, residing at—— " '

'Oh, cut the legal jargon, Peter !' urged Maisie. 'Look—down here is where it really starts.' She pointed at the place and went on reading aloud herself. ' " . . . do hereby leave and bequeath everything of which I shall die possessed to my nephew William McFlannel and I appoint him my sole executor—— " ' Maisie paused for breath and her aunt took the chance to nip in with :

'There—whit did Ah tell ye ! There's been durty work somewhere.'

'You shut yer trap !' ordered her husband with no noticeable sweetness.

Maisie read on : ' " For the following purposes (1) The erection

of a tombstone to my memory and for the maintenance in per-
petuity of my grave the sum of five hundred pounds." ' When
the ensuing pandemonium had flared up and died down again,
Maisie went on, ' " (2) the payment of the following sums :
(a) One thousand pounds to the Old Maids' Home——" '

' Eh ? ' gasped everybody except Willie.

' " (b) One thousand five hundred pounds to the Corporation
of the City of Glasgow for the erection and maintenance of a
pond for goldfish in one of the Public Parks." '

' Goldfish ! ' ' The woman's mad ! ' ' She shoulda had 'er
heid looked ! ' ' Whit aboot ma puir wee weans ? ' ' It's a
durty shame, so it is ! ' were some of the remarks called forth
by section (b).   Section (c) was found to be :

' " One thousand pounds to the person, man or woman, who
shall be in attendance upon me at my last illness." '

' An' who wis that ? ' asked several of the company.

' The meenister,' said Willie calmly.

' A black stranger ! ' was Geordie's amazed comment.

' There cannae be much left,' observed his wife.

' " Fifty pounds to the Dog and Cat Home." '   Maisie let
her glance travel down the remaining copperplate handwriting,
and then announced that as the residue went to her father, there
was nothing more to be read.

Mr. George McFlannel closed his eyes and made a rapid
mental calculation, announcing at last, ' Huh—Ah make that
fifty—eighty—eighty-one pound. No' bad, Wullie. Ah could
be daein' wi't masel'.'

Willie pointed out that the funeral expenses came to about
fifty pounds, which item of information drew forth the remark
from Mattha that it must have been a swell funeral. He, in turn,
averred that he could be doing with the remaining ' thirty pound
—odd.'

' The lawyer's bill came tae that ! ' snapped Willie.

' What ! ' gasped Sarah, her bright visions receding. She had
got to the stage where she no longer minded showing her feelings
in front of her in-laws. ' Thirty pounds is an awful lot for a
lawyer.'

'Ay—did ye no' know it costs ye ten an' sixpence every time ye nod tae a lawyer? Look—' Once again Willie fetched something from his pocket. 'Ah've got the account here—imagine! —thirteen an' fourpence fur whit they ca' " a lengthy telephone conversation "—that wis the day Ah got the man in the post office tae phone an' tell the lawyer it was time Ah wis gettin' back tae ma wife an' weans. An' here's anither thing. . . .' He was warming to his subject, but suddenly his audience decided that they were no longer interested in the details of the lawyer's account. Most of them were on their feet when he exclaimed, with feigned disappointment, 'Aw, are yez fur away a'readies?'

Mrs. George shook her head, glad of the opportunity to point out the shortcomings of her husband's relations, 'Ah don't know hoo Ah'm gonnae live doon the disgrace o' this—insanity in ma man's faimly!'

Mattha, conscious of the jibe, sought to nullify it by asking Willie if he didn't intend to contest the Will.

'Ach, Ah cannae, man! The lawyer said it wis watertight.'

In a steady stream the visitors poured out into the lobby and on to the stairhead, their journey having proved unnecessary and their hostess neglecting to see them off the premises. She sat down as the last claimant for Old Auntie's fortune left the kitchen.

'Oh dear-dear!' she moaned. 'What a night this has been! I don't know what the neighbours'll think. Thank goodness they're not *my* relatives! Open all the windows, Peter.'

As Peter rushed to obey her, Willie came back from saying good-bye to his kinsfolk. 'Puir auld Serah!' he said, slapping her playfully on the shoulder. 'Ye've had a bad time o't—but cheer up, ye never died a winter yet.'

'Don't talk like that!' she snapped. 'Four thousand pounds thrown away—down the stank!'

'Well——' Willie lit his pipe with a spill torn irreverently from the lawyer's account. There was a twinkle in his eye as he added, 'Well, no' quite four thousand.'

'How?' gasped Sarah, having noticed the twinkle.

'That thousand pounds the meenister shoulda got—he widnae take it.'

Maisie and Peter gathered round to share in their mother's astonishment. Willie went on :

'He said it wis against 'is conscience or somethin'. In fact, we'd a rammy ower the heid o't. But Ah made 'im take haufers fur 'is kirk.'

'So you've half of it left, Dad ! Five hundred pounds !' They all gaped at one another. 'Good old Dad ! I say—let's look for another house !' The suggestion came from Maisie.

Sarah, however, saw other plans for the money. 'Willie !' she fawned on him. 'Five hundred pounds ! Surely you'll not grudge me a fox fur now !'

But Peter had to put in an application too. 'I say, Dad, I heard to-day about a chap that's selling off his car—dirt cheap, it is. Imagine the fun we could all have if we'd a car.'

The idea immediately put all notion of the fox fur out of his mother's mind. 'Oh, a car !' she exclaimed. 'That would be lovely ! The M'Cottons haven't got one !'

Willie felt it was time to take a hand in the restraining of such wild schemes : 'Away wi' ye—the lota ye ! The money's a' spent.'

The consternation that appeared on the faces of his wife and son and daughter almost made the man giggle. He waited for the shock to spend its full force.

'Ay,' he went on in grim satisfaction. 'Ah bocht Savin's Certificates an' things wi't.'

His nearest and dearest looked at one another. There was nothing they could do about it.

'Come on,' said Willie, taking advantage of their silence. 'Don't staun' there gapin' like stuck pigs. Whit's fur ma supper ?'

CHAPTER 9

THE PATCHWORK QUILT

ONE evening a few weeks later Willie and Sarah were in the house by themselves, Willie sitting puffing contentedly at his pipe, and nursing the dog at the same time. Lassie was an old lady now, who could no longer leap on to his knees, but had to be lifted gently ; in consequence she was all the more valued. When Sarah came into the kitchen with a large cardboard box Willie wanted to know what was in it.

' The makings of a patchwork quilt I've been working at for years. It's for Maisie—I'm sure you've seen me at it hundreds of times ! '

' Ach, Ah didnae recognize it in its new box. Ah've aye meant tae ask ye—whit wey are they a' different colours ? '

' Because it's a *patch*work quilt, silly ! As my old grannie used to say, " Fools and bairns should never see half-done things." '

' Wid ye no' a' been quicker tae of stitched big swatches of cloth thegither ? '

' Of course it would've been quicker ! ' returned Sarah, ' but this is more artistic. Look—all the pieces are the same shape— six sides—and I've made exactly eight hundred and sixty-four pieces. I'm ready to join them together now. I'll just empty them on to the table and sort them out roughly into a design.' She upturned the cardboard box and began to rummage among the multi-coloured hexagons. ' My ! Some of these bits of cloth bring back memories. See, Willie, here's one made out of my wedding dress.'

Willie squinted at the article held out for his inspection. ' Whit—that blue thing ? ' he queried.

' It's not blue—it's helio. I never met a man yet that had an eye for colour.'

' Wis ye no' mairrit in white ? '

106

The casual manner in which the question was asked infuriated Sarah.

'Willie McFlannel!' she stormed, 'd'you mean to tell me you've forgotten what your wife looked like on her wedding day?'

'Jeengs, Serah, Ah havenae forgotten ye were jist a wee bit skelf o' a lassie. Whit weight are ye noo?'

Once again he had asked the wrong question and in the wrong manner. 'Oh, shut up!' said Sarah. She herself relapsed into silence until her continued rummaging brought to the surface another piece of cloth which she held up. 'Look, Willie, there's a wee patch made out of Polly's first walking frock. It was a real bonnie wee dress, that.'

Willie, however, was not at all interested in the cast-off garments of his children. 'Hae ye ony patches there made oota ma auld semmits?' he inquired.

'Don't be ridiculous. There's nothing but silk or satin used for this quilt.'

'Ah wonder,' he commented thoughtfully, 'whit it must feel like tae've sat -in a silk semmit. Eh, Serah? Ah said—Ah wonder whit——'

'I heard you the first time,' was the scathing retort.

Just then Maisie returned from one of her frequent outings in the company of one or other of her many boy-friends. When she opened the kitchen door and saw the heap on the table she wanted to know what the mess was.

'Maisie!' exclaimed her mother in hurt surprise. 'It's your patchwork quilt.'

'Oh,' said Maisie flatly.

'Ay,' put in Willie, 'she says there's four hunder an' sixty-eight pieces there.'

'Eight hundred and sixty-four!' snapped Sarah in correction, 'and I'll thank you not to make a fool of me!' Her tones were weepy as she went on, 'I've been working my fingers to the bone for the last three years on this quilt and this is all the thanks I get!'

'Oh, Mother,' protested the girl, 'I never said a word!'

'You called it " the mess on the table " ! '

'But—but . . .' Maisie fumbled for the right words to say to a mother who seemed to be in a touchy mood to-night. 'I'm sorry ! I say—some of the patches have fallen on to the floor. I'll pick them up for you.'

'No—leave them where they are ! ' Sarah sniffed back a tear. 'I'm trying to sort them into a design. I tell you what— I'll go and get an old sheet and I can lay them on that on the floor.'

When she had left the kitchen, Willie said, 'Ay, Maisie, ye'll be as prood as a dug wi' twa tails when ye pit that in yer bottom drawer.'

'Oh yeah ? '

'Ye don't sound awful enthusiastic ! '

'Maybe not ! '

'D'ye no' like the thing ? '

'I loathe it ! ' said the girl with intensity.

'But—but yer mother thinks it's awful braw.'

'I know. I hate to hurt her feelings, so I just sing dumb. But Dad, it's going to be the ghastliest thing you ever saw. That sort of quilt is out of date now. If ever I get a home of my own, I want everything to be just the last word. Nothing old-fashioned or make-do-and-mend. I could weep when Mother goes all sentimental about this blue bit being her wedding dress and——'

'It wisnae blue ! ' interpolated Willie remembering his own mistake. 'It wis helio.'

But Maisie, knowing nothing of the lesson her father had just learned, snapped, 'Now don't *you* get all sentimental ! '

Sarah came back just then, carrying the dust sheet which she spread on the floor. She had pushed back table and chairs, one of them with her husband and dog in it, when the door-bell rang.

'My goodness ! ' she exclaimed. 'Who'll that be ? Just when I was hoping for a quiet evening to ourselves. You go, Maisie ! ' As the girl went away, Sarah called after her, 'And if it's Mrs. McMuslin up the stair, tell her I can't lend her a wee tate of anything.'

Sensing that his wife needed some humouring, Willie offered to help her to spread the patches on the sheet, but once again he had said the wrong thing. 'Just you stay where you are!' he was told. 'I've never yet seen you put your hand to anything that you didn't make a hash of. My goodness! Listen! That's a man's voice at the door. He's coming in! Who can it be?'

'The wee Insurance man?'

'No—he was here yesterday.'

At that Maisie flung open the door and announced that her Uncle Matt had arrived. Instantly Willie was on his feet to welcome his brother, and the warmth of his greeting made up for the chilliness of Sarah's attitude. Always rather ashamed of her husband's people, she particularly disliked Mattha for his lack of straightforwardness, his hang-dog appearance, his Irish wife, his perpetual poverty and thriftlessness, and, above all, his adenoidal rendering of the Glasgow dialect.

'Come in, come in!' exclaimed Willie in spite of the fact that Mattha was coming in, albeit burdened by the weight and cubic measurements of the case he was carrying. 'Whit's this ye've got?' added Willie. 'Are ye traivellin' fur dolls' eyes an' railway tunnels?'

'Naw. Ah hope Ah havenae came at an awkward time.' The hope was expressed in the general direction of Sarah, as though to placate her. Sarah, for her part, declined to encourage the hope.

'Put your suitcase at the end of the bunker,' she said.

In order to reach the end of the bunker, Mattha had to negotiate the dust sheet spread on the floor, with the patches scattered upon it like confetti. 'Ah'm sorry tae be trampin' ower yer sheet,' said he, 'are yez spring cleanin'? Ah widnae of came if Ah had of knew.'

'Naw!' said Willie, taking a hand in the safe deposit of the case. 'Sit doon, man. Sit doon. Serah's makin' a patchwork quilt. She's made six hunder an' forty-eight six-sided pieces.'

'Eight hundred and sixty-four!' The correction came from the quilt-maker herself.

'Imagine that!' commented Mattha adenoidally, as was his wont.

'I was asking Uncle Matt just now if the size of his suitcase

109

meant he was coming to spend a holiday with us, but he's not giving away any information,' said Maisie.

'Ugh, never mind that the noo,' said Mattha evasively. 'Ehm—Serah—some o' thur bits o' cloth are rale bonnie.'

A little of the chill was gone from Sarah's manner as she replied, 'D'you think so, Mattha? Look—here's one made from the first pair of baby's shoes Maisie ever had!'

'Imagine that!' exclaimed Mattha once more. 'My, that reminds me of an awful nice bit poetry Ah seen in the paper the night. It wis aboot a baby that died——'

'Look here, Mattha McFlannel!' said Sarah firmly, seeing through his antics, 'you didn't come here to-night to talk about patchwork and poetry. Come on—out with it.'

'Ugh, there's nae hurry, Serah. Ehm, Wullie—hoo are ye gettin' on at yer work thae days?'

'Fine, man. Fine. Ah've got anither hauf-dizzen men.'

'Imagine that!'

This time it was Willie who tried to fathom the mystery of their visitor's call. 'Whit's in the suitcase?' he asked point-blank. 'Have ye left the wife?'

'Naw-naw. Naethin' like that. Ehm, Maisie—hoo's the school gettin' on?'

'The School, thank you, was quite well when I left it at four o'clock this afternoon.'

Undaunted by the frigidity of the tone, Mattha continued, 'Is it boys or lassies ye're teachin', Maisie?'

'Both.'

'Imagine that!' For a moment or two he seemed at the end of his string of conversational red herrings, then he brightened up, saying, 'Is Peter no' in the night?'

'Peter's oot winchin'!' declared Willie inaccurately, and before Sarah could correct the statement Mattha had come away once again with his:

'Imagine that! My, it seems jist like yesterday that Ah wis learnin' 'im tae play fitba' on the Saut Waste.'

Said Sarah, 'I'll thank you, Mattha McFlannel, to keep your mouth shut about those days.'

'Ach, Serah,' put in Willie, 'keep yer hair on. There's better folks nor us stertit in a room-an'-kitchen. Ehm—Mattha—aboot yer suitcase here—is it no' ower near the fire?'

'Naw-naw. It's fine. Is she a nice lassie?'

'Is wha a nice lassie?'

'Peter's girl.'

'Here!' exclaimed Sarah. 'That's enough about us. Come on, Mattha! Out with it! Are you, or are you not, up for the lend of money?'

'Oh well, ehm, no' exactly. Ah mean—Ah widnae pit it jist, well, jist so direc' as that.'

'Well, I can tell you before you start begging—you're not getting a brown penny out of us. I've been hearing things about you. Come on, Willie, back me up.'

Willie looked uncomfortable as he temporized, 'Well——'

'Now, Willie, none of your hunker-sliding. You know perfectly well what'll happen if you give Mattha money. If it was *my* brother, now. . . .'

'But,' Willie's excuse came lamely, 'he hasnae asked us fur the len' o' onythin' yet. Have ye, Mattha?'

Before Mattha could agree, Sarah nipped in with, 'Not yet—but he's going to. All that soft soap about how you're getting on at your work. I'm surprised at you, Willie, not seeing through his dodges.'

Willie looked at his brother sitting on the other side of the fireplace, his elbows on his knees, cap in hand, the picture of crafty humility. 'Come on, man!' he urged. 'Can ye no' speak up fur yersel'? *Are* ye wantin' the len' o' money?'

'Well, no' exac'ly. . . .'

Maisie, in the background, murmured a derisive 'Imagine that!'

'Ye see, it's like this——' began Mattha.

'I know!' said Sarah, also in derision. 'Your wife's needing new shoes. Well, I'm needing new shoes too. See?'

'Ach, Serah, gie'm a chance tae speak fur 'imsel',' pleaded Willie.

'Huh—and let him pull the wool over your eyes! Let me

III

tell you, Mattha McFlannel,' she shook a forefinger before the eyes of her wretched brother-in-law, ' you're getting no money out of us. Your wife is better dressed than me. . . .'

'Than I, Mother,' said Maisie schoolmarmishly.

'That's right,' responded Sarah missing the point, ' or you either, Maisie. And what's more, I know for a fact she's——'

Willie got to his feet. ' Will you shut up, Serah ! ' Turning on his brother, he demanded, ' Mattha—are ye, or are ye no'—wantin' the len' o' money ? ' all over again.

'Well, as a matter o' fac',' Mattha, twirling the cap in his hand, avoided the eyes of his brother, ' Ah wis hopin' fur tae maybe kinna persuade yez tae let me hae a fiver tae the en' o' the month.'

'There you are ! ' exclaimed Sarah triumphantly. ' What did I tell you ! Well, I've said my say, Willie, and if you dare to put your hand in your pocket, I'll—I'll—leave this house to-night.'

Treating the threat with the nonchalance it deserved, Willie faced up to his brother again. ' Ye're gettin' intae the habit, Mattha, o' dodgin' up tae me every time ye're on the rocks. D'ye no' mind the last time ye promised ye'd pey me back in a fortnight, an' Ah've seen neither hilt nor hair o't.'

Without giving Sarah time to ask her husband why she had not been told of these financial transactions, Mattha, his timid oiliness leaving him, blurted out, ' Och, but this is different, Wullie. This isnae jist an ordinary len' o' five pound Ah'm wantin'. Ye see, it's like this.' He threw down his cap in his enthusiasm. ' Ah've got somethin' here in ma case fur tae show yez.'

'If you're trying to sell us something,' Sarah warned him, ' you needn't bother opening it.'

'But Ah'm no' tryin' fur tae sell it tae *youse* ! ' said Mattha picking up the case and snapping it open. The family peered in amazement as he brought out a weird contraption, the chief feature of which seemed to be a box-like device with a large rubber hose attached.

'Whit is't ? ' asked Willie. ' A gas-mask fur an elephant ? '

Disregarding the patches which had all this time lain neglected on the floor, Mattha hauled and tugged at his exhibit, till Sarah had to protest and plead with Maisie to help her to lift her precious eight hundred and sixty-four hexagons of silk and satin. Together, mother and daughter piled the patches on to the table, where they lay in neglect while the attention was once again riveted on Mattha.

'It's an invention,' Mattha explained in open pride. 'A' outa ma ain heid. Ah want tae let ye see hoo it works. But ye'll need tae pit yer fire oot.'

'What !' blurted out Sarah. 'Put the fire out on a cold night like this !'

Willie, for his part, wanted to know what the heck this contraption had to do with the loan of five pounds.

'D'ye no' see ?' complained Mattha, disentangling himself from the affectionate rubber hose, 'Ah'm wantin' tae patent this. An' Ah need five pound mair nor whit Ah've got the noo.'

'But what's it for ?' demanded Maisie.

'Wait tae Ah tell ye !' With the back of his hand, Mattha brushed away an enthusiastic slaver from his mouth. 'Yez've a' heard o' vackyum-cleaners fur carpets an' things—well, this is a vackyum-cleaner fur the grate. See ?'

'Of all the daft-like notions !' was Sarah's comment.

Willie said, 'Ah'm feart, Mattha, ye're barkin' up the wrang tree if ye think Sarah'll pit the fire oot fur ye tae gie a demonstration.'

'Shouting down the wrong lum, in fact,' put in Maisie.

'Och, but there's nae need fur tae pit the fire oot, reely,' explained the inventor. 'See—everythin's lined wi' asbestos, so if ye jist lift aff the biggest bits o' coal, Wullie, Ah'll show yez hoo the thing works in a jiffy.'

Willie's instinctive move towards the grate was halted by his wife. 'Leave those tongs alone, Willie ! This kitchen's newly cleaned, and I'm not having any jookery-pokery.'

'Ach, Serah, gie Mattha a chance,' pleaded the hen-pecked husband. 'Ye never know—maybe it'll work !'

'Of course it works !' insisted Mattha in aggrieved tones. 'The wife thinks it's a bobby-dazzler !'

Sarah's contempt for Mrs. Mattha was such that she was constrained to say that in that case she had even less interest in the article than before. Mattha, however, ignored the remark.

'Have yez an electric plug handy?' he asked, peering into all corners and spying at last the plug intended for the electric iron. It was hailed as the very thing the doctor ordered. Sarah shook her husband by the arm.

'Willie!' she pleaded, 'are you going to stand there and see my nice clean kitchen all mucked up with this daft invention?'

'Sarah!' said Mattha as though swearing a solemn oath, 'if there's a speck o' dust on yer mantelpiece efter Ah'm feenished, Ah'll—Ah'll—clean it maself.'

'Oh, let him say his piece, Mother,' suggested Maisie.

'Well, listen you to me, Mattha McFlannel—even supposing your contraption works. Supposing it's the finest invention that ever came out of anybody's noddle—you're getting no money out of us—d'you hear me?'

'Och but, Sarah, surely ye'll let me show ye the thing workin'!' wheedled Mattha.

'Ach ay, Serah! Gaun!' wheedled Willie, in league with his brother.

'Look!' Mattha unravelled himself once more. 'This big nozzle is fur fittin' on in front o' the bars o' yer grate—see? Then this piece is fitted intae hit, an' the pipe is attached tae the motor—see? An' when ye switch on the power, the dust an' ashes is sooked doon this cylinder here intae the box. Hit's lined wi' asbestos forbye—see?'

When the explanation was complete and the rubber hose was round Mattha's ankles again, Sarah discovered a smoking lump of coal on the hob and proceedings were held up for a few minutes, while she accused her husband of sabotage on the home front. There was that in his eye that made her decide to let the demonstration go ahead.

'Ay, Mattha,' said Willie encouragingly and quite un-necessarily. 'Go on. Whit dae ye dae then?'

'Well, ye jist emp'y the cinders an' ashes an' stones intae yer ash-busket—see? An' it's ready fur takin' doon tae the midden —see?'

' All I can see,' Sarah declared witheringly, ' is that you're going to lose an awful lot of perfectly good cinders along with your ash. These days when coal's so scarce I pick every wee bit of black cinder out of the grate before I clean it in the morning.'

' Och ay, Serah,' said the inventor, ' but this thing'll no' be patented fur months an' months, an' by that time the war'll be ower an' coal 'll be mair plentifu'.'

' Months and months, did you say?' demanded Sarah. ' Then what about our five pounds that we were to get back in a fort-night?'

' Och well, that wis jist in a manner o' speakin'. If ye fling some sand on the fire, Wullie, it'll pit it oot quicker.'

Maisie decided to co-operate by fetching the bucket of ARP sand from the lobby press. She did so with the remark to her mother that she might as well give in now as later, as she was bound to do in the end.

' Oh, all right!' There was a sort of grudging resignation about Sarah's reply. ' But mind, Mattha, that doesn't mean to say you're getting a penny piece out of me, and that goes for you too, Willie. You're only encouraging him, standing there listening to all his balderdash. I've told you before, dozens of times, that if people can't save money themselves, they shouldn't come scrounging to other people who can.'

Maisie came back in a moment or two with the sand. The whole boxful was required to smother the fire, Sarah meanwhile standing well back, her hand clutching her jumper in an agony of foreboding. But amazingly there was no explosion, no disaster, no cloud of smoke even. Some of the tautness went out of her spirit as Mattha connected his brain-child to the wall-plug. Perhaps by some good fortune they would all come safely out of this visitation.

' Wullie,' commanded Mattha, ' you keep yer eye on the box —see? An' Ah'll attend tae the nozzle. Noo, is everythin' tightened up? Nae loose couplers nor onythin'?'

Maisie pointed out that some of the cinders in the grate were still red-hot, but Mattha turned aside this warning with the reminder that his container was lined with asbestos. Declaring that he was now 'all-set,' he switched on the current and rushed to the fireplace, where he held the huge nozzle in front of the bars ; in a moment or two the grate was empty of sand and cinders, there was a smell of hot rubber, and a triumphant Mattha turned a face flushed with heat and excitement to his sister-in-law.

'There !' he yelled above the din of the electric motor, 'whit did Ah tell ye ? Come on an' see !'

Sarah unhooked her grip on her jumper. 'Maisie !' she exclaimed, 'nothing's happened. No accident or anything ! Oh dear-dear, I can't believe it ! Let me sit down.'

Mattha, wiping his forehead, laid the nozzle of his mechanical device on the table.

'Oh, Uncle Matt !' protested Maisie. 'I shouldn't put that on the table. It'll dirty the patches for the quilt.' And she made to remove it.

'Naw it'll no',' retorted Mattha with considerable indignation. 'Feel it—it's no' even warm !' Maisie felt—with a timid forefinger. It was just as the man said—not even warm. He was irritatingly pleased with himself. 'Whit d'ye think o't, Serah ? It works—does it no' ?'

'Oh, it seems to work all right,' was the reluctant admission.

As for Willie, he was completely diverted and full of admiration for his brother's achievement. 'Jeengs, Mattha, that's a great contraption ! Whaur's yer ash-bucket, Serah, an' Ah'll emp'y this box an' Maisie can take it doon tae the midden.'

Sarah, mindful of wartime scarcity of coal, said that she would get the ash-bucket, but that it was not going to the midden until she had recovered every piece of combustible cinder.

'An' ye made this up oot yer ain heid, Mattha ?' continued Willie in delighted wonderment.

'Ah did that !'

'An' the electric motor forbye ?'

'Well, ehm——' Mattha hedged a little. 'Ah got hit oota an auld vackyum.'

'Ah'll jist switch it on again tae Ah see hoo it works,' said

Willie, adding as the motor moaned into action, 'Is there nae fear o' stertin' a fire in this box-thing when the air's gettin' sucked in ? '

'Naw,' yelled Mattha above the noise of the motor. 'Pit aff the switch tae Ah let ye see a wee dodge Ah've pit in the cylinder.'

Sarah disappeared to fetch the ash-bucket as Willie, Mattha and Maisie bent over the invention to examine its perfections. When she came back she wanted to know where Maisie had put the makings of the patchwork quilt.

'I never touched them' said the girl. 'I thought you had taken them away yourself.'

Sarah looked at the empty table, at the empty cardboard box, her mind refusing to admit the solution of the disappearance of her treasures, but the evidence lay before her eyes, clamant for recognition. 'Mattha !' she accused with something of terror in her voice, 'what have you done ? '

'Ah nun-never done nothin' ! ' replied Mattha, aware of the terror but not the reason for it.

'My patches ! ' shrieked Sarah. 'They're down that vacuum of yours ! In that box ! With all the red-hot cinders ! Oh—— Oh——'

'Help ma boab ! ' yelled Willie, all his sympathies now on the side of his suffering wife. 'Quick, Mattha ! Open the box ! Come on, man. Are yer fing-ers a' thoombs ? '

'Ah'm being as quick as Ah can ! ' insisted the inventor. ' But it wisnae me that switched it on the noo. It wis you, Wullie, d'ye no' mind ? '

'Never mind who dun it. Get the box open. It wis you that left the nozzle on the table, ya durty galoot.' Catching sight of Sarah's desolate face, Willie ordered Maisie to take her mother away for a few minutes.

Maisie, in spite of her antagonism to the future patchwork quilt, was quick to see the despair in her mother's heart ; she led her away lovingly and without any resistance from the patchmaker. As the door closed on the two women the men tried not to hear the haunting cry :

'All my work ! Years of it ! All gone up in smoke ! Oh Maisie——'

Left alone, they managed to get the noisome box opened, and in a moment the air was clouded with the smouldering of eight hundred and sixty-four pieces of silk and satin. The grate was deemed to be the best place for it—sand, cinders, and all. Conscious that he was partly responsible for the disaster, Willie felt some measure of sympathy for the manifold sorrows of his brother, married as he was to an Irish termagant—a slut who would never dream of making a quilt ; poor Mattha, thought Willie, he's got no steady job——

'Here, Mattha,' he said aloud, putting his hand into his jacket pocket and drawing out a battered and ancient railway timetable, 'afore Sarah comes back—here's a coupla quid. Ah'm sorry Ah cannae gie ye ony mair. But mind—never let dab tae Serah.'

'A coupla quid !' Mattha gaped at the money being pushed into his hand. 'That's real decent o' ye, Wullie. Ah'll gie ye it back, as sure's daith.'

'Ach, forget it ! Come on—let's get this fire goin' again ! Jeengs, Ah wid never 'a thocht that eight hunder an' sixty-four patches wida got wasted as quick as a' that. Yer motor must be awfu' strong.'

'Ay. Oh ay. Ehm—Wullie—it wis jist a coupla quid Ah wis needin', but Ah thocht if Ah asked fur five Ah wid maybe get twa. See ?'

Willie saw. Mattha, he recognized, had always been a bit of a twister, but recriminations would be postponed until the fire was set going. The door opened.

'Dad !' said Maisie, 'Mother wants to speak to you. She's lying down on the settee in the sitting-room.'

'Och, whit's up noo ?' demanded the man as he left the kitchen, dusting his hands on the lining of his jacket and closing the door after him softly, almost furtively and wholly apprehensively.

'Uncle Matt !' whispered Maisie. 'Quick ! Take this !' She thrust something into the inventor's not-too-hesitant hand. 'I'm sorry it's not more. But don't tell Dad or Mother.'

Once again Mattha gaped at the spectacle of money lying in his palm. 'Three quid!' he jerked out. 'Ma conscience!' His conscience thus summoned unwittingly, he made a tentative protest, 'Ah—Ah cannae take it, Maisie.'

'You take it!' said the girl gruffly. 'And keep your trap shut! It's a sort of thank-offering for not having to shove a patchwork quilt in my bottom drawer.'

'Imagine that!' was all that Mattha could ejaculate as he poked the three pound notes into his vest pocket beside their two predecessors. 'Here!' he came to life again, 'help me tae get this thing back intae ma case, Maisie. Ah'd better be oota here afore yer mother comes back.' Urgency was added to their efforts as the sound of footsteps reached them coming in their direction. The door opened.

'Oh, it's jist yersel', Wullie,' said Mattha in relief. 'Ah thocht Serah was wi' ye. Ah'm jist goin'.'

'Ah think ye'd better, Mattha. Here, Maisie—yer mother wisnae wantin' me at a'! She wisnae even in the sittin'-room when Ah went tae look fur 'er!' Maisie appeared too intent on assisting her uncle to reply to her father. 'Well, ye're away, Mattha. Guid luck tae ye! So long. Mind whit Ah tellt ye, noo!'

'Ah'll mind!' promised Mattha obligingly. His farewells were somewhat perfunctory as he manœuvred himself and his suitcase out of the house and down the stairs. Willie and his daughter faced each other in the kitchen.

'Whit wis yer mother wantin' tae see me aboot?'

'How should I know? I say, Dad,' continued the girl confidentially, 'isn't it marvellous about the patchwork quilt being destroyed! I can scarcely believe my luck.'

The door opened and Sarah came in, all the hopelessness gone from her manner. 'Is that man away?' she demanded.

'Ay. Look here, Serah, it wis a pure accident . . .' began Willie, when Maisie, catching sight of what her mother was carrying over her arm, interrupted with :

'Hullo, Mother, what are all the dresses for? You're surely not thinking of going away for a holiday?'

'These are out of the rag-bag!' Sarah informed her, placing them one by one on the table. 'I'm going to cut them up.'

'Whatever for?' asked Maisie, foreboding in her heart.

'For another patchwork quilt, of course. I'll join the patches together as I go along this time.'

Maisie left the kitchen hurriedly to hide her chagrin. Three pounds 'down the stank,' she told herself. And another patchwork quilt to haunt her future. Oh well, maybe she would never be married; after all, some old maids had a pretty jolly time of it, no responsibilities, no inventive in-laws. . . .

CHAPTER 10

'FOUR FEET ON THE FENDER'

A FEW worrying weeks went by and Sarah was moving round the house trying to persuade herself that she was not really missing Lassie. She avoided looking at the bare patch of linoleum at the side of the grate where the dog's basket used to be ; true, the leash still hung on a peg on the hallstand, but you didn't need to go into the lobby very often. It was ridiculous to be upset over the death of an old dog ; Lassie had been done and doitered for ages—it was time she was put to sleep. But in spite of all her arguments, Sarah was feeling a sense of bereavement and loneliness. Lassie had been a grand excuse for talking to herself, a wonderful safety-valve when she was boiling with wrath over her husband's social *gaucheries*. Continuing to mope over the loss of Lassie, Sarah got to the stage where she would have welcomed a visit from Mrs. M'Cotton. When the door-bell rang, therefore, she rushed to open it, and her delight was great when she discovered her visitor was her old friend Mrs. McLeather.

'Come away in !' she exclaimed in welcome. 'Must you rush away or can you wait a wee while ?'

'Oh, I'm not in a terrible hurry,' conceded Mrs. McLeather, 'I just felt it was such a time since I'd seen you, and it was such a nice afternoon, I couldn't stay away any longer.'

'Well, come on into Maisie's room and take off your things.' Sarah led the way, asking, 'How are you keeping ?'

'Not bad at all, thanks. I really can't complain. What about you ? Everybody well ?'

'Oh, we're well enough,' Sarah admitted with a grudge. 'I mean, none of us is ill or anything like that.' She scrutinized her friend's clothes. 'Is that a new hat ?' she asked. 'It fairly suits you.'

Mrs. McLeather took off the headgear with the suggestion that Sarah should try it on herself.

' Oh, I don't know,' protested Sarah smoothing her hair. ' I don't think that style would suit me. My face is so fat. I tried on·one of Maisie's that was that sort of shape, and Willie said it looked like a pea on top of a drum.'

' Ugh, but husbands have no idea what suits their wives,' said Mrs. McLeather comprehensively. ' All *they* want is for us to look as inconspicuous as possible. Come on—try it on.' Sarah was not too difficult to persuade, and in a moment the hat was on and Sarah was adjusting it this way and that to find a comfortable perch for the morsel of felt and ribbon. Mrs. McLeather, her head on one side, frowned. ' What about putting it a wee bit more to the side ? ' The result was just as unsatisfactory. ' Uhha,' she conceded at length, ' it maybe *is* a wee bit on the small side for you.'

Sarah plucked up enough courage to look in the mirror. What she saw made her gasp. ' Oh, did you ever see anything so silly in all your life ! D'you know,' she went on, taking the hat from her head in disgust, ' it's a nightmare for me to go and buy a hat. My face is so fat ! I could weep every time I look in a mirror.'

' Get away with you, Mrs. McFlannel,' the visitor was in duty bound to protest. But Sarah paid no heed. She went on :

' Willie says he could weep too. He says *I* don't need to look in a mirror unless I like, but *he's* got to look at my face whether he wants to or not.'

Mrs. McLeather replied uncomfortably, ' Yes, but you know what Mr. McFlannel is—he must have his little joke. He doesn't really mean to hurt you.'

' That's what *you* think ! ' retorted Sarah with some bitterness, then, remembering her duties as a hostess, she added, ' Here, never mind doing your hair—it's fine. Come on ben to the kitchen and we'll have a cup of tea. I baked a wee cake this morning.'

' Any new recipes ? '

' Oh, lots ! Cakes without fat, without eggs, without sugar

even. My goodness, Mrs. McLeather,' she went on, leading the
way to the kitchen, 'don't you get fed up with the whole
business ? '

'Oh, now and again. And soon we'll be expected to make
them without flour ! Talk about making bricks without straw.'

'Here you are,' said Sarah. 'Sit down here beside the fire.
My sister that's living in Aberdeenshire sent me a cake last week.
She made it herself with farm butter and shell eggs. I've still
got a wee bit left to let you taste it. I'd forgotten cakes tasted
like that. Willie says if I'm putting on weight when food's so
scarce in Glasgow—what would I be like if we lived up north.'

Mrs. McLeather, unsuspecting that she was about to act as
substitute for a rheumaticky, blind, deaf old dog, said, 'I think
you're a wee bit down in the dumps to-day, are you not ? You
don't usually take to heart what your husband says.'

'Maybe I *am* a wee bit depressed,' admitted Sarah wielding
the kettle and teapot.

'Have you any idea what's making you like that ? '

'Oh, just everything, I think.'

'Such as ? Or would you rather not talk about it ? You
know you can trust me, don't you ? '

Sarah nodded a mute agreement.

'Well, then. . . .'

'It's. . . .' Sarah halted—tragedy, grief, disillusionment,
despair weaving a pattern across her face. 'It—it's Willie that's
worrying me.'

'Good gracious !' gulped the amazed Mrs. McLeather.
'Whatever's the matter with him ? Don't tell me—I mean—it's
not drink, is it ? '

'No-no !'

'Then—is it money difficulties ? '

'No, it's not that either. Oh, I don't know how I'm going to
tell you.'

'Surely,' protested the visitor, 'at his age—it's not . . .
wu-women !'

'No-no-no ! I sometimes wish, though, that it was !'

Mrs. McLeather got up from her chair by the fireside, and came over to where her friend was standing by the table. Putting an arm round Sarah's shoulder she shook her gently, saying, ' Don't talk nonsense ! That's the worst thing that can happen to any wife ! ' Suddenly she abandoned the shake in favour of a squeeze as she went on tenderly, ' Come on, Mrs. McFlannel— tell me what it is. It'll do you good to open your mind about it to somebody. Is it—I mean—he hasn't been dishonest, or anything like that ? '

' No, it—it's worse than that ! ' Sarah gulped.

' Save us all ! What on earth . . .' Mrs. McLeather pulled Sarah round to face her, gripped her by both shoulders, and demanded, ' Here, come on—out with it ! '

Sarah sniffed, swallowed hard, sniffed again and, a tear trickling down her cheek, she blurted out, ' It's—it's—well, it's just nothing ! '

' Nothing ? But you've just said . . .' Mrs. McLeather's patience seemed in danger of wearing thin.

' Yes, I know.' Sarah dabbed at her eyes and looked round for a seat. ' Oh, I wish I knew how to tell you. But that's the trouble—there's nothing to tell.'

' Then I just don't see what——'

' Oh, you don't understand. Maisie's got her friends—she's out every night in the week. Peter's out every night too— classes and things. And that means, now that Willie's not going out to the Home Guard so often, that we just sit by the fire our two selves.'

' Bu-but I don't see anything wrong with that ! '

' You don't ? Well, I'll tell you. Willie gets his paper—he reads it all during tea-time, of course, but that's not enough. Oh, no. He's got to read it all over again by the fireside. From beginning to end. And if I speak to him he just grunts. When I've been in the house alone all day I want somebody to talk to in the evenings. Some nights I'm so fed up I could scream.'

' But I thought you went out canteening.'

' No. I had to give that up. Blood pressure, I think.'

Mrs. McLeather stared in bewilderment for a bit, then she said, ' Well, then, Mr. McFlannel can't read the paper *all* evening. Even the advertisements wouldn't take more than an hour.'

' Ugh,' disgustedly, ' he goes to sleep then.'

' The man'll be tired after his day's work.'

And, in spite of all the warnings she had received on the point, Sarah came out with her old chestnut of unconscious humour, ' Work ? He doesn't work—he's a foreman ! '

' Well, supposing ! What do you want him to do ? Take you out to the skating rink, or something ? '

' Oh, if you're going to make a fool of me——'

' I'm sorry ! ' The apology came with real sympathy. ' I didn't mean to do that. All the same, Mrs. McFlannel, I do think you're making a lot of fuss for nothing at all. You should be thankful your man is a sit-by-the-fire instead of gadding about with a younger woman. He's just at the age when they take notions for that sort of thing, you know. And to my mind, that's the last indignity a woman can thole.'

Sarah flared up at that. ' And do you not think there's any indignity in being treated as if you were a piece of furniture ? I sometimes wish I could take ill or something—just so's he'd miss me and be glad to see me when I came home again.'

' Oh, you mustn't say that ! Why not go out yourself in the evenings ? '

' But where could I go ? I'm not keen on the pictures or the theatre or anything like that. And as for traipsing about to other folks' houses—well, I'm just not that kind of woman.'

' What about joining a club of some kind ? '

' Oh, but I couldn't barge in among a crowd of strangers ! ' Then, remembering about the tea she had made, Sarah added, ' I say—do you take sugar ? '

' No, thanks. Well here—what about getting up a club amongst our own friends—a sort of unofficial Red Cross work party. We could meet, turn about, in one another's houses.'

Sarah thought about the suggestion for a moment or two before giving a hesitant, ' Well—maybe. It might be quite a good idea. I've got to the stage where I'll try anything rather than suffer another night by the fire with Willie.'

'Well,' went on Mrs. McLeather, accepting a piece of Sarah's home-made cake, 'who do you think we should ask?'

'Not Mrs. M'Cotton anyway,' declared Sarah, 'that woman rubs me the wrong way.'

'I'm sure Mrs. McVelvet would like to join.'

'Uhha? How many d'you think we'd need?'

'Oh, about six, say.'

'That's other three we want. I had an old neighbour—a Mrs. McTweed. She's not what you might call out of the top drawer, but she's a dab hand at cutting out patterns. I tell you what—we'll have a sort of preliminary meeting here—say some night next week. Would Tuesday suit you?'

'My word—you're a fast worker! Yes, Tuesday would be all right.'

'And we'll make it a rule that there's just to be a cup of tea and a cookie or something—but nothing fancy.'

'Good idea, but of course——' But what reservation Mrs. McLeather was going to make to the plan was hastily squashed by Sarah, who went on:

'I suppose we'll need funds to start with. Well—I'll give a pound.'

'Splendid! But——'

'I've got an old pair of curtains that would make up into bedjackets.'

'But what will Mr. McFlannel say to all this?'

'Oh, him!' Sarah dismissed her husband's opinion with a sniff. 'He'll be too wrapped up in his newspaper to notice whether I'm at the other side of the fire or not. Now, what about——'

Sarah's newest suggestion, however, was doomed never to be uttered, for at that moment the door-bell rang. With a tut-tut of annoyance she hurried to the door. There she found a policeman. Her first thought was of Matt; she hung on to the door-handle for moral support.

'Are you Mrs. McFlannel?' asked the policeman.

Sarah's 'yes' had to be swallowed, but her nod indicated what she meant to say; there was a gravity about his face she interpreted to mean bad news. Oh Matt, she mourned, my bonnie wee Matt. Had it been a submarine? Or a floating mine? She clamoured for, yet dreaded, further information.

'You've to go to the Infirmary at once,' said the man in blue.

'Oh! So he's not drowned after all!'

The policeman looked at her in bewilderment, then went on to explain that he was merely a messenger, that he knew no more than that Mrs. McFlannel was to go to the Casualty Ward where her husband lay, following an accident at his work. Leaving the man standing on her doormat, she rushed back to the kitchen, screaming:

'Oh, Mrs. McLeather! Fancy! Willie's met with an accident. I'm to go to the Infirmary at once.'

'Oh dear me! Is it serious?'

'It must be, or they wouldn't have sent for me.'

'Well—away you go and get on your hat and coat. I'll come with you.'

'That's awful kind of you!' In a dither, Sarah clutched at her friend. 'Oh dear—I wonder if——' She broke down completely, sobbing, 'Oh, I can't bear to think of it.'

'Now don't you start imagining things!' said Mrs. McLeather, patting Sarah's shoulder. 'Just you get ready.'

'Just fancy,' Sarah dabbed at her eyes, 'he's wearing the awfullest old pair of underthings—all patched and darned, they are! What'll the nurses think?'

'If I know Mr. McFlannel, he'll be keeping the nurses laughing so much they'll not have time to notice his underwear. Come on—hurry up.'

'I'm hurrying as fast as I can,' replied Sarah, running hither and thither aimlessly. 'Oh dear—I wish the policeman hadn't been so stupid. He didn't seem to know anything about Willie. They might have more consideration for relatives.'

'But the policemen don't have anything to do with the hospital. The nurse on duty just phones the police to get in touch with the relatives. You'll just need to be as patient as you can till you get there.'

'Patient? How can I be patient and my man maybe lying

cut to pieces ? Oh dear—I never thought I'd live to see this day.' With admirable restraint Mrs. McLeather refrained from reminding Sarah of her attitude towards her husband only a few moments earlier, but when Sarah suggested putting on an old waterproof for the journey, her friend thought it time to take a hand.

'No, you won't ! You'll put on the best you've got in your wardrobe. The nurses will notice what you're like if Mr. McFlannel doesn't. And don't look on the gloomy side—maybe it's only a slight accident, and——'

Sarah stopped on her way to the wardrobe to say, ' How could it be a slight accident if they've sent for me ? Oh—what about Maisie and Peter ? Would they not be better to be there too ? '

' I'll go for them myself if we find Mr. McFlannel's awful bad.' Together they went again into Maisie's room where Sarah kept her clothes. Putting on her wisp of a hat, Mrs. McLeather examined her hostess. ' Yes, I like you in that black coat—but not with blue woollen gloves.'

' Oh, never mind my gloves.'

' Look ! ' From an open drawer there peeped a pair of green gloves. The visitor pounced on them. ' Here's the gloves Maisie got to match your green handbag and your hat. That would be better.'

' Oh—I couldn't wear my green hat ! My grannie always used to say, " Out of green into black." '

' You and your grannie ! That's pure rubbish ! Come on ! You look real lady-like in your green hat ! '

Simply because it was going to be less trouble to agree, Sarah put on the green ensemble, and, having made sure that the gas was out under the cooker, the two women hurried out to the Infirmary a few streets away. They were directed to the Casualty Ward, Sarah assuring her friend over and over again of her gratitude for her company ; together they hung round the door of the ward until a nurse came within hailing distance.

' Excuse me, nurse,' said Sarah, remembering to speak carefully, ' but is this the ward my husband's in ? '

'What's his name ? ' was the casual query. Surely, thought

Sarah, none of her patients can be very bad or the nurse would look more worried.

'McFlannel. William McFlannel. He met with an accident at his work.' Somehow the words seemed to form themselves in spite of the agitation in her throat.

'Oh yes?' Still casual, the nurse went on, 'Just come this way, will you?'

'I'll wait outside here for you, Mrs. McFlannel,' whispered Mrs. McLeather. 'I'll keep my fingers crossed for you.'

With a nod Sarah followed the nurse, almost slipping on the polished boards of the floor as she hurried to make up with her and ask:

'Is he—awful bad, nurse?'

'Not at all! He's had slight concussion. A rivet seems to have fallen on his head—fortunately he was wearing a bowler hat at the time, and it saved him from worse injury. He's been unconscious for a bit, but he's coming round now—— There he is,' she added, indicating the second last bed. 'You mustn't wait more than five minutes—and try not to excite him.'

'Thanks, nurse.' All at once Sarah was reluctant to approach her husband. 'D'you think he'll know me?' she asked.

'Oh, I'm sure of it!' said the nurse, smoothing her white apron over her hips. 'He mistook me for an angel in heaven a short time ago, but he's improved since then.' A dimple appeared at the corner of her mouth and a twinkle in her eye indicated some inner amusement. 'Now remember—five minutes only!'

Sarah was left alone to complete the rest of her journey across the shining boards. She reached the bed indicated and stood holding on to the iron rail at the foot of it, scarcely able to make out her husband's face owing to the tears that dimmed her eyes. In any case, the man's head was swathed in a bandage, making him look pitiful and defenceless and unfamiliar. 'Oh, Willie!' she gulped quietly. 'Willie!'

The man looked at her and said, 'Uh.'

Growing bolder she left the foot of the bed and went nearer the bandaged head, oblivious to the other beds, to the other patients, to the slatternly woman sitting at the next bed watching her grimly.

'Oh, Willie!' she repeated tenderly, a world of shame and love and gratitude in her voice. 'My own darlin'.'

'Uh,' said the patient again.

'Do you know who it is?' she asked. 'It's me—Sarah.'

'Whit wis that ye said?' came the feeble croak.

'I said it was me—Sarah.'

'Ay, but afore that—whit did ye say?'

His eyes were closed, so she could not see if there was the familiar glint in them whereby she knew she was being teased. 'Before that?' she murmured. 'I—oh Willie—dud-darling——' She swallowed a sob bravely.

'That wis it! But Ah don't deserve it.'

'Don't deserve what?'

'Tae be in heaven.'

'But you're not in heaven, dear,' Sarah assured him, squeezing the flaccid hand on the coverlet.

'Ay, but Ah am!' Willie insisted weakly. 'It's heaven jist tae hear you ca'in' me yer darlin'—Ah didnae know angels wore green hats.'

His flippancy in face of what might have caused his death made Sarah's tears all the more eager to fall. She tried to smile them away. 'Willie!' she said brightly—then 'Willie!' this time more urgently for a change had come over the man. 'Willie! Speak to me! Willie!'

From the side of the next bed the slatternly woman grunted, 'Ach, he's unconscious again, missus. Ye cannae dae onythin' aboot it. Here's me been sittin' waitin' here fur the last two hoors waitin' fur ma man tae come-tae. An' tae tell ye the honest truth, missus, Ah don't ken whit Ah'm waitin' fur 'cos we'll jist stert rowin' a' ower again as soon as 'e comes roon.'

Sarah stared from her unconscious husband to the woman, uncertain whether or not to engage in conversation with such a slut. Still, a common bond of affliction was binding them together in this cheerless ward.

'Has your husband had an accident too?' whispered Sarah.

'Accident ma fut!' answered the woman, not whispering. 'He fell aff a larry. Tryin' fur tae get a hurl fur nothin', an' the driver widnae slow doon fur tae let 'im aff. Wait tae 'e comes roon', an' Ah'll caw the buits aff 'm, an' me in the washin'-hoose the day.'

'Is he badly hurt?'

'Hoo should Ah know? It's a durty shame, so it is, an' hit sichna grand day fur dryin' blankets. Whit's up wi' your man?'

Sarah made sure she was not neglecting her husband before turning to the woman again. 'The nurse said it was slight concussion. A rivet fell on his head at the work, but his hat saved him from being worse.'

'Is 'e a foreman?'

'Yes—in a shipyard.'

'Ach, it's aye the same. Some o' the men 'll've been tryin' fur tae crown 'im.'

'What do you mean!' demanded Sarah indignantly. 'It was an accident.'

'Sez you! Heh—look—he's comin' roon' again.'

And so he was, for he was groaning, 'Oh ma heid, ma heid!'

'Poor Willie!' murmured Sarah, bending over him. 'Is it awful bad? Have you been crying? Your eyes are terribly bloodshot.'

'Whit wey am Ah lyin' on a slab?' he inquired huskily.

'You're not lying on a slab! You're in a bed.'

'Well, it feels like a slab. Whaur am Ah?'

'You're in the Infirmary. You've had an accident. Something fell on your head at the work.'

'Ah could dae wi' a smoke.'

'Oh, you're not allowed to smoke in the Infirmary.'

The slut at the next bed, however, had apparently an extensive knowledge of hospital etiquette, for she assured Willie, 'Wait tae they shift ye up tae yin o' the wards up the stairs, mister. Ye can smoke in ablow the blankets when the nurses isnae lookin'.'

'Ah'm maybe lyin' on a slab,' commented Willie, 'but Ah don't want to be a smoked herrin'. Heh, Serah, Ah don't mind o' comin' in here. Was Ah brung in a Black Maria?'

'You mean an ambulance ? I expect so. But I don't think you should try to talk, dear.'

'Say thon again, Serah.'

'Say what ?'

'Ye ken fine, lass.' He pawed the air. 'See's yer haun'.'

Sarah grasped the wandering hand in her own. 'Here you are, Willie. I'm here beside you.'

'Don't leave me. Ah'm awful—kinna—sleepy.' With that he had lapsed into unconsciousness again, greatly to Sarah's distress, a distress that was observed by the lady at the adjacent bed.

'That's him away again,' she pointed out unnecessarily. 'He's been daein' that fur hauf an hoor. The first time 'e wakened up, 'e tellt me tae cheer up Ah never died a winter yet.'

'Did he ?' The phrase that had irritated her for so many years merely made Sarah smile tolerantly now. 'Isn't that like him !'

'Are yez no' long mairrit ?' asked the woman.

'Why ?'

'Talkin' love tae yin anither like that——'

'We've been married about thirty years,' said Sarah.

'Eh ?' was the incredulous ejaculation.

'Wid ye mairry me again, Serah ?' came the wobbly voice of Willie.

Before Sarah could reply the slut exclaimed with mournful satisfaction, 'Ach, the puir sowl's ravin' again.'

But to show he was not raving, Willie repeated the question, this time with a gentle pressure on the hand that held his. The pressure was returned.

'I would that, Willie,' came the assurance.

'An' go through everythin' jist the same as it wis ?'

'Just the same.'

'Ah cannae see ye !' he complained. 'Staun' a bit nearer . . . that's better . . . ye—ye're awful bonnie, lass.'

'What !' gulped Sarah. 'Me ? Bonnie ? With my fat face ?' Ignoring the cynic a couple of yards away, Sarah flopped down on the chair at her husband's bedside, and, weeping unashamedly, she sobbed, 'Oh, Willie !'

'Ay.' The man chose not to see the tears. 'An' yer eyes

132

are jist as bricht as they were when we were coortin'. D'ye mind Ah used tae ask ye tae get lichtin' ma pipe at them?'

'Ach, you're an awful man!' she whispered, sniffing.

'An' d'ye mind Ah used tae write wee bits o' poetry aboot them?'

Once again the fountain of Sarah's tears was let loose. 'I—I'd fuf-forgotten that!' she confessed.

'Ah've made up anither piece, lass.'

'Have you?' she asked in amazement. 'When did you do it?'

'Och—sittin' at the fireside at nights when there wis jist you an' me in the hoose.'

'Oh, Willie,' she managed to say by way of expressing disgust at her own lack of perception.

'Ah cannae mind it a' the noo,' he went on, unaware of all the shades of meaning in her utterance, 'but Ah've got it written doon on a wee bit paper in ma pooch. Whaur's ma jaiket?'

The fact that the woman at the next bed had heard all their conversation was clear when she said:

'Look in the locker at the side o' 'is bed there, missus. Sometimes they pit their belangin's oot their pooches in theym.'

Sarah soon found the locker and the jacket and the pocket in question. She fetched its contents out one by one.

'What's here?' she wanted to know. 'A watch, a knife, two dirty hankies! Oh, Willie, why didn't you take a clean hankie this morning—of all mornings!' But she couldn't be vexed with him for long. 'Some money. A pocket-book. Is it in here?'

'Ay, but it's no' jist polished up yet, mind,' said the poet.

'The paper's pretty dirty.'

'Ay. Ye see Ah've been cairryin' it aboot wi' me, tryin' tae make it better. But maybe ye'd raither wait an' read it at hame?'

'No—I'll read it just now.' Lowering her voice, she stumbled over the pencilled words:

'"When seated by the fire at nicht,
    I look—an' there's ma bonnie lass!
Her een that glint wi' inward licht
    Are dimmed na by the years that pass."'

She got no further; her voice choking with renewed self-recrimination, she said, 'Fancy you writing such lovely poetry about me. I'd no idea . . . you felt . . . like that. . . .'

'Here, whit's up wi' ye?' demanded the man. 'You're a fine yin—come in tae see yer man's corpse in the Infirmary an' ye never bat an eyelid, an' then ye read a bit poetry an' ye burst oot the greetin'.'

Wiping away her tears, she retorted, 'I'm thinking you're the fine one too! Here you are—might have been killed and you're quite joco. And when you've got a cold or a pain in your tummy you're up to ninety-nine.'

She put the scrap of paper carefully in her handbag, saying she would read the rest when she got home.

'Don't go away, Serah!' he urged, with an invalid's querulousness.

'But I'll have to, Willie. The nurse said I was just to have five minutes. Is there anything you'd like?'

'Naw. Jist yersel'. Ye're a sicht fur sair een.' There was a moment's silence, then he murmured, 'Serah.'

'Yes, love. What is it?'

'Nothin'. Jist "Serah," Serah.'

He closed his eyes, and the woman at the next bed shook her head, saying, 'He's goin' unconscious again. That's a bad sign.'

This Sarah stoutly denied, insisting that he was only dropping off to sleep, but the woman knew better:

'Naw, 'e's no'. Ah mind when Ah had ma operation fur ma perspirated stummuck, there wis a wumman in the next bed that wis aye drappin' intae unconsciousness like that, an' she wis deid in hauf an hoor.'

'Oh, don't say that!' pleaded Sarah, with a frightened look at her husband's eyelids.

'Have ye ony faimly?' asked the woman.

'Yes. Four.'

'Whaur dae ye stey?'

'Oh,' evasively, 'out Partick way.'

'Ah've got a sister steys in Dumbarton Road. Maybe ye'll know 'er. . . .'

Without waiting to remind the woman of the length of Dumbarton Road and the multiplicity of its tenements and the inhabitants thereof, Sarah smiled triumphantly as she exclaimed, ' Oh—he's all right. He squeezed my hand just now ! '

The nurse came forward just then, saying :

' Well, Mrs. McFlannel, I'm sorry but you'll have to be going. Your husband is looking very much better.'

' Here,' demanded the watcher by the other bed, ' whit aboot *ma* man ? Can ye no' gi'e 'im a clout on the jaw or somethin' tae waken 'im up ? Ah've got ma washin' tae feenish. . . .'

Willie, however, felt he was losing some of the publicity he deserved, so he demanded, ' Can Ah get up noo, nurse ? Ah feel like a cod in a fish-shop windae lyin' here on this slab.'

' Oh, you'd better not get up just yet ! ' said the nurse, with the dimple threatening to appear any moment. ' We'll see how you are in the morning.'

Said Sarah, ' You'll not keep him in any longer than you need to, will you, nurse ? '

' You can be sure of that, Mrs. McFlannel.'

' Whit's fur tea, nurse ? ' asked Willie, true to form in spite of the bandage. ' Ham an' eggs, wi' a wee bit finnan haddy ? '

' Wait and see,' she temporized, sending at the same moment an eyebrow signal to Sarah that she would have to leave at once.

' Well, Willie,' said Sarah, getting to her feet and bundling her damp ball of a handkerchief into her handbag, ' I'll need to go. See and behave yourself now, and not be saying cheeky things to the nurses.'

' Are ye no' gonnae gie's a wee cheeper ? ' he asked in disappointment.

' Ugh, you're an awful man ! ' All the same she bent down, with a smirk of triumph aimed at the cynic, and kissed her man heartily, satisfyingly. ' Now,' she whispered, ' you hurry up and get well, and I'll have something nice for your tea when you come home.' Reluctantly she followed the nurse out of the ward, inquiring, *en route*, when she might be able to have her husband home. The nurse's opinion was that he would be well enough to travel the following day.

'Oh, good!' said Sarah. 'I'll be here for him with a taxi.'
She paused at the door to look back at the second last bed in the
row. 'Oh, nurse, look at my husband! Sitting up waving to
me! The rascal! Oh dear, what'll the other patients think—
him blowing kisses to me like that!'

The dimple appeared in real earnest, and remained to make a
pleasant accompaniment to the nurse's statement that Sarah was
a very lucky woman to have such an affectionate husband.

'It's me that knows that,' Sarah assured her. 'Well, bye-bye,
nurse, and thank you for being so nice. I've always been a bit
afraid of nurses, you know.'

At the door Mrs. McLeather greeted her friend anxiously.
'How is he?' she asked. 'One of the nurses was telling me a
rivet fell on his head.'

'Oh, he's wonderful,' said Sarah rapturously, and yet so
ambiguously that Mrs. McLeather looked aghast.

'Here, what's come over you?' she demanded. 'You're
looking a different woman.'

'Oh, I'm awful relieved, that's all,' said Sarah, trying to
dowse some of the glory in her face.

'D'you know—your eyes are shining like—like a girl in
love!'

'Ugh, get away with you, Mrs. McLeather.'

Together they made for the Infirmary gate, and having
satisfied herself that her friend's husband was in no danger,
Mrs. McLeather said at length:

'I say—I was just thinking while you were in the ward—
about this Work Party. . . .'

'What Work Party?' asked Sarah politely, if indifferently.

'Good gracious, don't say you've forgotten! The one we
were going to get up because you were sick to death of sitting
at home with your husband.'

'Oh, that? But—but that's all off.'

'Is it? Why?'

'Well, you see—I—ehm—there's nothing I'd like better than
to sit at the fireside again with Willie—just our two selves.
"Four feet on the fender."'

'Well, I never!' gasped Mrs. McLeather, 'so it took a falling rivet to knock some daylight into your noddle! I'm real glad, all the same.'

They made a detour to visit a tea-room; Sarah reckoned that the cake made with farm butter and shell eggs had better be reserved for the sole use of the returning casualty case the following day.

CHAPTER 11

MATTHA CLOCKS IN

THE following Saturday afternoon Sarah was out shopping, and the returned casualty case, complete with head bandage, was left at home with Maisie, who was fussing over her father to such an extent that the man had to protest he had been in the Infirmary only a couple of days and not a couple of years.

'Oh, I just wanted to let you know I was glad you were home again, Dad!' said Maisie, packing a cushion behind his ear. This brought his head round so that he had an uninterrupted view of nothing but the pulleys and the kitchen clock high up on the frieze.

'Here!' he exclaimed, 'whit's up wi' the clock? It's ten meenits slow! Whit has yer mother been daein' wi't when Ah wis away—a spring cleanin'? It never went slow afore! Ah'll need tae hae a look at it.' Then, realizing that as a patient with a bandaged head there might be some restrictions on his movements, he added cautiously, 'When d'ye think yer mother'll be back?'

'Depends on the length of the queues, I expect. Why?'

'Well, Ah don't want tae vex 'er by makin' a mess.'

'Heavens! What's come over you two? You're like a pair of love-birds since you came home, Dad. Oh, here—if that clock is slow I'll have to hurry. I'm going out.'

But before she got the length of the lobby the door-bell rang and, on going to investigate, she discovered that her uncle was on the doormat, ostensibly to pay a call on his invalid brother. Maisie ushered him into the kitchen, where he was received with immediate cordiality by Willie.

'Well, I'll leave you two alone, Dad. I'm going out,' said Maisie.

'Right ye are! Tell 'im Ah wis askin' fur'm.'

'Tell who?'

'The chap ye're goin' oot wi'.'

'Oh, Dad!' protested Maisie, 'you've got a one-track mind.'

She was gone in that instant, and Willie turned to his brother, saying, 'Sit doon, man. Sit doon. Take aff yer bunnet an' make yersel' at hame.'

'Ah wid be mair at hame if Ah wis tae take aff ma buits,' replied Mattha with the usual nasal stop in his melancholy speech. 'Ma corns is botherin' me somethin' terrible.'

'Well, take aff yer buits if ye want tae. Serah's no' in—an' Ah'm used wi' bad smells at the work. Did ye hear Ah'd met-in wi' an accident?'

'Ay,' replied Mattha casually, as he applied most of his attention to the removal of his boots. 'Ah jist said tae the wife "Ah'll awa' oot fur a dauner an' cry in at Wullie's in the by-goin'," but Ah near turned back efter Ah wis hauf roads here —ma corns wis giein' me jip.'

'D'ye tell me that,' said Willie, with as much concern for his brother's afflictions as Mattha was showing for his. 'Ay—Ah wis in the Infirmary. . . .'

'Ouch!' yelped Mattha, wrenching off one boot. 'Naeb'dy has ony idea o' the agony ma corns gi'es me. Ah've yin atween ma big tae an' the next yin. Oh! That's a relief! Ah'll jist take the ither yin aff forbye.'

'Ay,' continued Willie, refusing to be side-tracked, 'it wis a rivet that fell on ma heid. Ah had concussion.'

'Imagine that! Well, Ah widnae like tae think o' a rivet drappin' on my corns. Ah've got yin on the sole o' this fut—the wife says Ah'm shammy-leggit wi' tryin' tae save walkin' on it.'

'Ach, ye were aye shammy-leggit, Mattha,' said Willie with a brother's brutal frankness. 'Ah've got tae get this bandage off on Monday.'

'Imagine that!' said Mattha, at work on his other boot. 'Well, Ah've had a bandage on this corn here fur six weeks. Ouch! That's the ither buit aff. Ouch! Ah can see better noo. Corns is a terrible tribulation.'

'D'ye tell me that! Ye should see the corn Ah've got on the tap o' ma heid whaur the rivet dunted me.'

'Here!' exclaimed Mattha callously, 'is yer nock stopped?'

'Naw, but it's ten minutes slow. Ah wis jist gonnae take 'er doon fur tae ile 'er when ye came in.'

'Ah'll gie ye a haun'. Ah know everythin' aboot nocks. Ah've jist feenished sortin' yin fur the man next door.'

'Is it keepin' time, but?' asked Willie, with a suspicion born of his knowledge of Mattha's inefficiencies.

'Oh well,' Mattha hedged, 'ye cannae expec' a slap-up job fur jist ten shillin's.'

'Well, Ah'll get the steps f'ae the lobby press,' announced Willie in the absence of any of his family to do the job for him. As he came back into the kitchen with the article in question Mattha once again offered his assistance.

'Naw, staun' back!' ordered Willie. 'Noo here—it's jist ile that the clock needs—so ye neednae be coontin' on ony ten shillin'ses f'ae me!' He spread the steps and prepared to mount them.

'Whaur are ye gonnae lay the nock?'

'On the table there. You take yer bunnet aff it. Ah ken it's greasy, but it's no' that kinna grease Ah'm fur pittin' on the clock! Here—haud the steps, man, till Ah get the clock aff the nail.' To the accompaniment of the jangling of the interior bell, Willie added, 'That's the worst o' thae wa' clocks, they're sichna bother tae take doon when onythin' goes wrang wi' them.'

Mattha at the foot of the steps was ready to receive the clock from the hands of his brother at the top. He held it poised for a moment while he was warned to exercise the utmost care in placing it on the table. That done, and Willie once again on the floor, Mattha was further instructed:

'Noo, you haud off. Ah can manage this masel'. Noo whaur's the machine ile?'

'A wee tate paraffin is best, Wullie. If folk only kent it, a wee daud o' cotton wool soaked in paraffin ile an' left hingin' near the works wid save them f'ae an awfa lota watchmakers' bills. Ye should try it.'

Deciding to take advantage of his brother's amateur advice,

Willie went in search of the paraffin, throwing over his shoulder the threat :

'If you touch that clock, Mattha, Ah'll set fire tae yer shirt tail !' He snocked about in the scullery demanding of no-one in particular, 'Noo whaur's that paraffin ile ? Here's an auld mulk bottle fu' o' somethin'.' He sniffed. 'Smells like paraffin. Oh ay—here's the label. Whit wis that ye said aboot cotton wool, Mattha ? '

Mattha, however, failed to reply to the question, for at that moment his attempt to turn the clock face round proved rather unsuccessful. There was a crash of breaking glass as it bumped on the table.

'Oh heh, don't look at me like that, Wullie !' yelled Mattha. 'It wisnae ma fau't. Ah wis jist turnin' 'er roon', so's we could get at the works. Oh help ! There's gless a' ower the place. Ah hope Ah don't get ony, an' me in ma stockin' soles.'

Willie's wrath found expression at last. 'You're the shirt an' semmit, Mattha ! Ah *tellt* ye tae lea'e it alane ! Well, that'll cost ye the ten bob ye were talkin' aboot.'

'Whit fur ? '

'Fur a new gless, man. Here—staun' oot the road till Ah get this swep' up ! Wait you tae Serah comes in an' sees whit ye've done. You'll get the benefit o' a' the rows Ah havenae been gettin' this last week.'

'Yow !' barked Mattha. 'Ah tramped on a bit gless the noo. Oh ma corn ! Oh ! Oh ! '

'Serves ye right, ya haunless gowk, ye !' stormed Willie. 'Could ye no' a' laid the thing alane ? '

'But it wisnae ma fau't,' wept Mattha. 'Oh, Ah'll hae tae sit doon. Ma puir corns ! '

As Mattha collapsed in self-pity into a chair Willie searched in all the most unlikely places for the brush and shovel, the latter of which he finally ran to earth in the coal bunker. Failing to find the brush, he announced that he would just use his brother's cap, which was still lying on the table.

'Naw, ye'll no' !' came the protest from the fireside chair. 'Ah'll maybe get gless in ma heid ! '

'Ye could be daein' wi't. Let some daylight intae yer noddle.'

'Aw, come aff it, Wullie,' pleaded Mattha. 'Ah'll try fur tae get ye anither gless. Although whaur Ah'm tae go fur it Ah don't know.'

The sweeping-brush was discovered eventually behind the scullery door, but it was wielded so inexpertly that Willie's temper burst forth into flame again:

'Ach, the gless is stottin' a' ower the place. It's your fau't, Mattha! Ya Hielan' stot—ye!'

Mattha, humbled, cringed into the chair, murmuring that as he had already said he was sorry, there was nothing more he could say.

Willie, shovelling some of the broken glass into the ashpan, went on grumbling, 'Ye're a glaiket sumph, so ye are! Jist you sit there, noo, an' don't move tae Ah've got the clock iled. Ah'll no' feel safe wi' ye tae it's on the wa'.'

'Ah wis only tryin' fur tae help ye, but!' protested Mattha. 'Ah wish Ah'd never came up tae ask fur ye!'

'Tae ask fur me?' repeated Willie in mock surprise. 'Ah didnae notice much concern tae hear whit Ah had tae say aboot ma accident.'

'Well,' Mattha fumbled for the right words, 'Ah—Ah came, didn't Ah?'

The fact being incontrovertible, Willie merely barked, 'Ach you! Whaur's the paraffin ile noo?' and when he had found it, Mattha plucked up the courage to ask by what means he intended applying it.

'Ach, Ah'll jist take the corner o' ma hankie,' said Willie.

'Ye'll hae tae be carefu' wi' a wide-necked mulk bottle like that, an' hit bung-fu' forbye,' pointed out Mattha, whose bravery was increasing with every moment. He managed to remain in his seat while Willie peched and chugged over the fastening of the back door of the clock. His breathlessness was further intensified by his explosive accusations that the cause of all the difficulty was his brother. The door eventually jerked open during one of Willie's unguarded moments, and when he had regained his equilibrium, he gaped at the dusty condition of the works thus revealed.

'D'ye no' clean it regular?' asked Mattha with the air of a patient parent with an oft-reproved child.

'Oh,' replied Willie, blowing away the cobwebs with spurts of breath and saliva, 'Ah whiles gie it a bit dicht.'

'Ye shouldnae spit intae it like that. It's bad fur the works.'

'Ah'm no' spittin'! Ah'm blawin'!' When he had puffed to his heart's content he proceeded to sprinkle some paraffin oil on to his least dirty handkerchief; Mattha, from his grandstand seat, found the waste of good oil so hurtful to his senses that he leapt to his feet shouting:

'Here—let me dae it! If ye gie the works ower much ile ye'll dae mair hairm than guid.'

'You lea'e me alane! Ah can manage fine masel'.' They struggled together for a moment or two with the slavering bottle between them until Mattha proclaimed:

'Gie it tae me! Ah ken faur mair aboot nocks than you dae!'

The struggle continued until the inevitable happened; the bottie, by now a rather slippery handful, fell out of Willie's grasp right among the works.

'Ya gowk ye!' yelled Willie. 'Skailt the ile intae the works.'

Mattha, however amateurish he might be, realized that greater damage had been done by the falling of the bottle than by the spilling of its contents, and he bethought him of his home. Indeed, he made an intimation to the effect that it was now high time he returned there. This hint riled Willie, who exclaimed:

'Ye're goin' hame nane—till ye've helped me tae pit this right. Jeengs—a hale pint o' paraffin inside the clock! Whit'll Serah say tae this? Help! It's dreepin' a' ower the place!'

'Oh! An' me in ma stockin' soles! Ah ay take the cauld in the heid when Ah get ma feet wet!'

'You shut up aboot yer wet feet!' roared Willie. 'Come on—gie's a haun'. Whit am Ah tae dae wi' this ile?'

'Whit aboot poorin' it doon the jawbox?' asked Mattha.

'An' choke the drain, maybe? Naw.'

'Well, ye cannae poor it on the fire fur fear ye set the lum on fire.'

'D'ye tell me that?' said Willie in derision.

'Ah know whit tae dae!' The inspiration came to Mattha joyously. 'Open the windae an' haud the clock oot ower the sill tae it dreeps itsel' dry.'

'Ay—an' hae the wife doon the stair up at me fur wastin' the floowers in 'er windae box?'

'Ach well—Ah wis jist tryin' fur tae help!' Mattha's justification broke off sharply as he began to yelp with pain and to dance about on one foot. In reply to his brother's query as to the cause of his behaviour, he explained: 'Ah musta tramped on anither bit gless. Oh help! Ma corns, ma corns! This is terrible!'

Willie's sympathy, however, was rigidly withheld as he himself danced around on both feet looking for some means of escape for the dripping oil. The tea-towel at the back of the scullery door proved a godsend; he mopped at the greasy pool, complaining that it would take a month of Sundays to complete the task, adding, 'Right anuff, Mattha, ye're a ham!'

'But it wisnae ma fau't, Wullie! It wis you—wantin' tae grab the bottle oota ma haun'.' Mattha paused in his hopping to examine the clock's interior more closely. 'Here!' he exclaimed mournfully, 'Ah don't like the look o' that mainspring!'

'Naw? Whit's up wi't?'

He shook his head. 'Jist whit Ah wis feart fur! The bottle musta broke it when it fell the noo.'

'An' hoo div ye sort a broken mainspring?'

'Ye cannae. Ye'll hae tae get a new yin.'

'Help ma boab! Whit next?'

'An' ye cannae get theym fur love nor money,' went on Mattha.

'That's torn it!' said Willie, flinging the sodden tea-towel on the floor. 'Wait tae Serah comes hame an' that'll be the end o' the honeymoon hur an' me's been hacin' thae past few days. That clock belanged tae 'er auld grannie, an' she fair worships it. Ach, *Ah could flype ye, Mattha.*'

'Ye can flype me if ye like,' commented Mattha calmly, 'but it'll no' dae ony guid. Av coorse, maybe ye could buy a new clock,' he added with a spurt of business energy.

'Whit ! Buy a new clock ! Ten meenits ago that clock there wis as guid as new.'

'Ah tell ye whit, Wullie,' said Mattha calculatingly.

Willie, knowing his brother's propensities, asked suspiciously, 'Whit noo ?'

'If ye liked, Ah could run across tae the Barras an' see if Ah could pick up a guid second-hand nock, an' we could take the mainspring oota it an' fit it intae this auld nock——'

'Hoo much wid that cost ?' demanded Willie with shyness born of experience. 'Ten shillin's ?'

'Och, Ah'm feart ye widnae get a very guid nock fur jist ten shillin's, Wullie. Three pound wid be mair liker it.'

'Three pound !' repeated Willie. 'Jeengs, Mattha, Ah'm no' *made* o' money.'

'Well, if ye want tae keep in wi' the wife, ye'll need tae dae somethin'.'

'Well, whit aboot you peyin' haufers ? It wis as much your fau't as mine—if no' mair. Ah'll gie ye thirty bob.'

With suspicious eagerness Mattha jumped at the offer. 'Right ye are ! Ah'll jist get on ma buits——'

'But whit aboot the paraffin ile in yer socks, man ? Will Ah get ye a clean pair o' mine ?'

'Ach naw. Ah've nae time fur luxuries. Ah'll away hame first an' get ma tea, an' then oot tae the Barras. Ah'll be back here aboot hauf-past seeven.'

'Well,' said Willie fumbling in his pocket with the air of a man being held to ransom, 'here's a quid an' a ten bob note, an' if Ah'm no' here when ye come back, ye'll ken Ah'm back in the Infirmary.'

'Whit wey ?'

'Och, Serah'll've gi'en me anither bash on the heid wi' 'er grannie's clock.'

Mattha ignored the remark, lacing up his boots as fast as he could. He got to his feet, blinked, and then ejaculated,

'Here—d'ye know—that paraffin ile's makin' ma feet feel better!'

'Ay!' came the bitter retort. 'An' noo that yer haun's greased forbye, ye'll be in gran' fettle fur the job. If Ah hadnae this bandage on ma heid Ah wid come wi' ye, jist fur tae keep an eye on ye. . . .'

'D'ye no' trust me wi' yer money?'

'Ach, it's no' the money that's worryin' me, although Ah could think o' better roads fur it. It's the wey you'll spend it.'

'Ah'll gi'e ye ma word fur it, Wullie . . .' began Mattha solemnly yet with urgency.

'Right ye are! Here's yer bunnet! Ye're lucky tae be gettin' away afore Serah comes hame.'

At that Mattha showed a certain reluctance to return later in the evening with his purchase; indeed he had so little desire to meet his sister-in-law that he was almost tempted to decline the commission.

'You'll come back, ma man!' commanded his brother. 'Clock an' a'! An' don't spend ony mair than ye can help.'

'Naw,' agreed Mattha, opening the door. 'No' a penny mair nur thirty bob.'

'Than three pound!' snapped Willie. 'You've tae pey yer whack tae, mind!'

'Oh ay. That's right. Ay. Three pound.' His voice faded away as he hurried down the stairs, and Willie went back to the kitchen to survey the damage and to compose his soul for the ordeal he knew lay ahead of him. Neither task was fully accomplished when, in a few minutes, Sarah came back from her shopping expedition. She came into the house complaining about the length of the queues, the incivility of shopgirls, the shortage of goods—but her husband, preoccupied with his own troubles, heard none of them. He took her shopping-basket from her as she remarked:

'By the way, I met your brother Mattha just now tearing down the road at an awful rate. Was he here?'

'Ay.'

'And how much was he up for the lend of this time?'

146

'He wisnae up fur the len' o' nothin'. He came tae see me.'

At that moment Sarah caught sight of a puddle forming at the door of the kitchen. Kilting her skirts unnecessarily, she exclaimed, 'My goodness! What's been going on here? The floor's all wet. And what's the clock doing on the table?'

'Och well, ye see——' began Willie.

The woman laid down her handbag on a chair. 'Willie McFlannel!' she said ominously, 'what have you and that brother of yours been doing?'

'If ye'd jist let me explain,' pleaded Willie uncomfortably, 'Ah wis gonnae ile the clock—it wis goin' slow——'

Just then the broken glass that Willie's perfunctory sweeping had failed to cope with caught Sarah's eye, and her thoughts leaped to the obvious conclusion; nevertheless she demanded, 'Don't tell me the glass is off the clock face!'

'Ay, but ach, it'll never be missed when the clock's hingin' up on the wa' again.'

'But where did the water come from?'

'It's no' water—it's paraffin ile!' Willie felt a little self-justification was necessary, so he went on in a synthetic temper, 'If you wid keep yer dusters in a place whaur folk could see them, Ah'd've had it dichted up by this time.'

Sarah ignored the temper as well as the accusation. 'Is that a dish-towel you've got in your hand?' she snapped. Then, remembering the happy relations that had existed between them since his accident, she almost broke down. 'Oh, Willie—and we were getting on so well together—and it my grannie's clock, too!'

'Aw, don't greet, hen!' All the insincerity, all the self-righteousness was gone from the man's voice as he went over and clapped his wife's shoulder. 'Ah'm awful sorry—Ah am that! Mattha's away fur a new mainspring—it'll be as guid as new again.'

Sarah's heart which had been softening at the beginning of his speech hardened once more. 'What!' she exclaimed, 'so there's more than just broken glass! Oh, Willie—it's awful hard not to give you a row. Really it is!'

'Ach, Serah, go on!' The man flung the duster and the basket of groceries down in sudden resolution. 'Gi'e's a row! Jist the same as ye used tae. Ah cannae staun' this honeymoon racket much longer.'

'If it had been anything but my grannie's clock,' wailed Sarah.

'Ay, Ah know.' Once again Willie was overcome by the sight of his wife's grief and the memory of his own clumsiness. 'Ah'm awful sorry, hen. But Mattha'll be here efter tea-time an' we'll can get it sorted.'

'Well, we'll see. . . .' She unkilted her skirts and picked her way with unnecessary care to the scullery. The sight made Willie smile so much that Sarah had to find out the cause.

'Ah'm mindin',' he confessed, 'aboot oor Mattha stottin' aboot in 'is stockin's holes tryin' no' tae jag 'is corns wi' the broken gless.'

The picture thus called up made Sarah snigger, and soon the pair of them were on the best of terms once more—a state of affairs that lasted until Maisie and Peter came home for tea; it even survived the usual Rangers-versus-Queen's Park partisanship that the BBC Sports Bulletin evoked. About eight o'clock Willie remarked that his brother was taking his time about returning with the second-hand mainspring for the damaged clock.

'Did you give him any money, Dad?' asked Maisie.

'Ay. Thirty bob.'

'Willie, you didn't!' cried Sarah with some incredulity and more vexation. 'You'll never see it again!'

'Ach, Mattha's maybe a wee bit through-ither, but he's honest anuff.'

'Through-ither? What on earth is that, Dad?' queried Peter.

'D'ye mean tae tell me,' demanded Willie, 'ye don't know whit through-ither means? Whit did they learn ye at the school?'

'*Teach* Dad!' Maisie made the correction in her normal schoolmistressy manner. '"What did they *teach* you at the school?"'

'Me?' inquired Willie. 'Ah wis *teached* at the school no' tae gi'e up cheek tae ma faither.'

When the door-bell rang nobody seemed anxious to admit the visitor. 'Ah cannae go,' said Willie, 'wi' this nichtcap o' a bandage on ma heid. It micht be Mrs. M'Cotton, an' she'd wonder whaur ma nichtshirt wis.'

Peter was finally persuaded to act as usher, and the first intimation the family received that all was not quite well was when they heard Mattha's voice.

'Heh, Peter,' he was saying with a vast amount of peching, 'ye'll need tae gi'e me a haun' wi' this nock.' The shuffling that ensued made Maisie suggest that it sounded as though they were bringing in a body. Even Willie got the length of going to the kitchen door and demanding to know what was going on. All the response he got was his brother's continued instructions to Peter, 'Easy-on, there. Ye'll hae tae up-end 'er tae get 'er in the kitchen door.'

Sarah, her hand at her throat, heard Peter retort, 'Well, don't shove so hard! Yow! You've snecked my finger!'

'Mattha McFlannel, what's this you're bringing in here?' demanded Sarah, joining her husband at the kitchen door.

But Mattha was still too intent on completing his flitting operations to reply directly. 'Jist a meenit, Serah,' he temporized. 'Heh, Peter—let 'er doon at your end. That's right! Noo, walk 'er in!'

'For Pete's sake!' ejaculated Maisie when the procession moved into her range of vision. 'It's a grandfather clock!'

'Willie!' gulped Sarah. 'Did you tell him to buy that old thing?'

'Ah did nut! Heh, Mattha—whit's the big idea?'

'Jist a meenit, Wullie. Ah'll tell ye efter Ah've brung up the waxcloth.' And before they could demand a further explanation, Mattha was moving out of the lobby in the direction of the common stairway, saying, 'Come on, Peter! You'll need tae gi'e me a haun'.'

'The waxcloth!' spluttered Sarah. 'What the——'

As for Willie, he suddenly forgot the possible misunderstanding that might seize Mrs. M'Cotton should she see his bandaged head; hurrying after his brother and son, he yelled down the staircase :

'Heh, Mattha ! Haud yer horses !'

But it was of no avail. He returned to the kitchen to hear Maisie saying that she had always wanted to collect antique furniture, but that this clock was worse than a ruin.

'Willie !' insisted Sarah. 'That brother of yours should be locked up ! What do we want with a grandfather clock—and such a shabby one too !'

'Well, ye see, the idea wis that if he could get an auld clock wi' a mainspring in it, we could take it oot an' fit it intae yer grannie's clock. But Ah don't see whaur the waxcloth comes in.'

'As far as I'm concerned, the waxcloth just *isn't* coming in !' replied Sarah firmly.

Maisie had meanwhile been inspecting the clock which she pronounced to be worm-eaten, and unsafe to have in the house for the sake of the rest of the furniture.

'Ach,' said Willie, his mind only half on the subject, 'we can break it up when we've got the mainspring oot. It's this waxcloth. . . .'

'But, Dad,' demanded the school-teacher, 'are you sure that the mainspring of a grandfather clock will fit a wall clock ?'

'Ach, stop argyin'. We'll jist hae tae make it fit.'

'Away you go, Willie,' said Sarah, 'and tell him he's not to bring any waxcloth in here.'

'Hoo can Ah—an' me no'-weel ?' asked Willie with the air of a martyr.

The point was still being argued, when the sound reached them of two men labouring under a weight.

'Oh dear-dear !' sighed Sarah. 'I do hope the neighbours aren't watching.'

'Heh, Mattha,' roared Willie from the kitchen door, 'jist you take that doon the stair again. We're no' needin' nae waxcloth.'

'Ah cannae dae that, Wullie,' panted Mattha. 'Ah've sent the man away wi's barra.'

'Man ! Barrow !' What on earth was this, thought Sarah, acutely conscious of her neighbour's opinions on the subject.

'Ay—ye see . . .' Mattha signed to Peter and they stood the roll of linoleum in a dark corner of the lobby. 'Ah couldnae cairry that big clock an' the roll o' waxcloth by masel', an' they widnae let me on a caur wi' them, so Ah jist asked one o' the chaps at the Barras tae help me.'

'Oh dear-dear !' sighed Sarah all over again. 'What *will* the neighbours think ! A barrow at the close !'

'But whit wis the idea o' gettin' waxcloth onywey ?' demanded the master of the house.

'Well, ye see, ye gi'ed me thirty bob, an' Ah managed tae get ye this dandy nock fur a quid,' explained Mattha, 'so Ah had ten shillin's left an' this wis a real bargain. Look '—he unfurled a corner of the linoleum and exhibited the design that had, after the manner of rolls of used floorcloth, been rolled downside-out—'in't it a braw pattren !'

'My sainted aunt !' gasped Maisie at the spectacle. 'It's the first time I've seen a picture of blood-and-toil-and-tears-and-sweat !'

'It looks like a bad accident to a zebra,' was Peter's impression.

'But you an' me wis goin' haufers,' protested Willie who had no aesthetic reactions, 'fur the clock ! Jist the clock ! Ye didnae need tae spend the hale thirty bob. That's fifteen shillin's ye owe me !'

'Fifteen shillin's !' It was Mattha's turn to protest. 'But—but——'

'Come on,' said Sarah, shoving Mattha closer to the unsavoury roll, 'just you away back to the Barrows with it !'

'Dae yez no' like it ?' asked Mattha in amazement.

'We don't like it ! We don't need it ! And we're not having it !' announced Sarah deliberately.

'Some kids might like it for making a back-court tent,' suggested Peter.

'Whit ! That braw pattren ! Ah'll take it hame first ! The wife wid be rale prood tae hae that on 'er fluir.'

'Right ye are, Mattha !' said Willie. 'That'll be twenty-five shillin's then.'

'Eh ?' gulped Mattha. 'It cannae be a' that !'

'Ay, but it is ! Ah gi'ed ye thirty bob, didn't Ah ? '

'Ay, but——'

'An' ye spent thirty bob ? '

'Ay, but——'

'An' we were goin' haufers ? In't that right ? '

'Ay, but——'

'Well, then, you owe me fifteen bob. But ye're keepin' the waxcloth that cost ten shillin's. Ten shillin's an' fifteen shillin's is twenty-five shillin's, in't it ? '

'Ay, but. . . .' Mattha was bewildered, benumbed and begrutten. Even Maisie was so amazed by her father's manipulation of the situation and the finances that she was forced into the exclamation :

'Talk about the three-card trick.'

'Listen, Dad,' began Peter. 'You're paying half——'

'Shut up ! Baith o' ye ! ' ordered Willie. Turning to his brother in the half-light of the lobby, he held out his hand, saying, 'Well, hand over the twenty-five bob, Mattha ! '

'Ah—Ah—but Ah gied the man a shillin' fur the len' o's barra ! ' protested Mattha.

'Well,' went on Willie with the manner of a benefactor controlling his impulses with difficulty, 'hauf a shillin's sixpence—that's twenty-five an' six ye owe me noo. Come on—oot wi't.'

'But, Wullie——' Mattha's moan was broken off as Maisie broke in with :

'I say, Dad, where were you *teached* that kind of arithmetic ? '

'You haud yer tongue ! ' commanded her father, continuing to hold out his hand to his brother. 'Come on, Mattha ! Twenty-five an' six ! '

Dumbfounded, Mattha blurted out, 'Thuth–that means that you're gettin' the clock fur—fur—four an' six ! It disnae seem right somehoo.'

'For goodness sake, Willie,' began Sarah.

'Look, Dad ! ' Peter attempted the impossible. 'Let me explain. You gave him thirty shillings——'

Maisie interrupted with the suggestion that paper and pencil ought to be furnished wherewith to illustrate the nefarious methods of their parent, and the ensuing dispute became so heated that at last Sarah shouted :

' Oh, my head's splitting. Listen, Mattha, if you'll only take away that awful waxcloth we'll say nothing about hauf—ehm—halfers.'

' But Ah want ma money ! ' roared Willie.

' Dad, look at it this way,' began Peter all over again.

' Ach, shut up ! ' snapped his father. ' Ye've got me a' flummoxed—the hale lot o' ye. Ah tell ye whit—you gie's the ten shillin's fur the waxcloth, Mattha, an' we'll say nae mair aboot it.'

' But whit aboot ma time an' expenses goin' tae the Barras ? ' asked Mattha.

' Anither word f'ae you, an' Ah'll make ye buy back the clock as well ! ' threatened Willie. ' Come on, clear oot—you an' yer smelly waxcloth.'

Grudgingly Mattha withdrew from his pocket a grimy note for ten shillings, saying, ' Ye're lucky tae be gettin' a braw grand-faither clock like that fur a quid, so ye are.' To Sarah's relief he shouldered the linoleum, and betook himself off. Willie there-upon eased the clock round in order to inspect the works. The sight of the pendulum and the weights reminded him of what he knew he ought to have realized before ; he felt, however, that Mattha's shoulders were broad enough to take the blame. Closing the clock door as quickly as possible, he dusted his hands and announced to his family :

' Ach, Ah mighta knew oor Mattha widda diddled us. There's nae mainspring in it.'

Maisie and Peter, by this time having lost interest in the transaction, merely murmured adenoidally, ' Imagine that ! ' and their mother was too exhausted mentally to chide them. When she had the energy, she told herself, she would insist on Peter and his father sawing up the old thing for firewood. In any case, since Mrs. M'Cotton had pointed out how old-fashioned wall clocks were, Sarah had been wondering how soon she could propose a mahogany one for the mantelpiece with (near) West-minster chimes. It was an ill wind. . . .

CHAPTER 12

CHRISTMAS CRACKERS

CHRISTMAS 1944. The war was plodding steadily towards VE-day; Matt, in spite of the incredible risks of his ship, was still safe and had been home recently. Matt—the round O—still remote and unpredictable, was an ever-present problem to his mother at home or at sea. Each spell in the bosom of the family seemed to emphasize his aloofness. Sarah grew increasingly aware of the fact that Matt would never again make his home with the family. Nobody knew what would happen when the war was over, but that much seemed fairly certain. They didn't seem to speak the same language. Not that Matt was unfriendly; on the contrary he went out of his way to be nice to them all, especially his mother. But that made no difference. Polly, living in Edinburgh, had given birth to a daughter, and as she was not making as good a recovery as had been expected, her mother had offered to keep five-year old Ian over the Christmas holidays while Maisie would be at home to look after him. And now, Christmas Day itself past, Ian in bed, Maisie and Peter due to come home any minute, Sarah ordered her husband to accompany her to the sitting-room.

'Whit fur?' asked Willie suspiciously.

'Because I'm expecting Mrs. M'Cotton to pay us a surprise visit, and I don't want her to catch us sitting in the kitchen.'

'But we aye sit in the kitchen, an' onywey, hoo can it be a surprise veesit if we ken she's comin'?'

'*She'll* mean it to be a surprise!' retorted Sarah, 'but I know the lady! She got a fur coat for her Christmas, and she won't rest till she's shown it off to me—just because *I* haven't got one myself.'

'Puir auld Serah! Ah'm sure Ah've said a hunner times—whit's tae hinder ye f'ae gettin' thon auld sheepskin rugs made intae a fur coat? They're lyin' in the room press there daein' nothin'.'

'And I've explained to you a hundred times—fur coats don't have hair six inches long!'

'Ye could aye stert a new fashion.'

'Ugh, don't be daft.'

'Well, ye could shave the rugs,' suggested Willie, as though anxious to be of assistance, but Sarah cut him off with a command to be quiet, as she thought she heard their grandson crying in bed. It was a false alarm, though, but Willie used the occasion to tease her about her fussiness where wee Ian was concerned, and, having exchanged views rather heatedly on the topic, they gradually worked themselves into a discussion on the relative claims of maternal and paternal grandmothers in general, and those of Mrs. McFlannel and Mrs. M'Cotton in particular. No conclusion appearing on the horizon, Sarah put an end to the matter by once again reminding her husband that she wished him to accompany her to the sitting-room, adding:

'And put on your jacket.'

'But Ah don't want tae pit on ma jaiket! Ah'm sure Jim M'Cotton sits aboot the hoose in 'is shirt sleeves as well as me!'

'Jim M'Cotton does nothing of the kind—his wife wouldn't allow him. And you take off those old slippers!' She thereupon produced another pair which Willie complained pinched his bunions, but Sarah this time won her point, and in a few minutes they were on their way to the apartment Willie called 'ben the hoose.' Passing through the lobby they encountered Maisie returning home, and the girl immediately demanded the reason for the procession. When she had been told, her father added:

'Ye better tell Peter when 'e comes hame that 'e's tae pit on 'is fancy slippers an' a flee-away collar. A lota palavers, that's whit Ah say!'

He was firmly manœuvred inside the sitting-room by his wife, who led him to an easy-chair, saying, 'There, now—isn't that a lovely fire! This *is* cosy!'

But Willie refused to sit down until he had fetched his pipe from the kitchen.

'No, Willie,' wheedled Sarah. 'See here—' she brought

forward a box of cigars. 'Smoke one of those, seeing Peter gave you them for your Christmas.'

'Ach—cigars!' growled Willie in great contempt. He fingered the things tentatively. Then something caught his eye. 'Here—Ah'm surprised at ye dryin' a washin' in this room if ye're expeckin' Mrs. M'Cotton.'

'What washing?' asked Sarah; then catching the direction of his amazed glances, she added, 'Oh, don't be silly! These are the new chair-backs I got from Maisie for Christmas. Leave them alone, you galoot!'

Willie replaced, wrong side out, the article in question, saying, 'Don't tell me antimacassars is in again!'

'They've been in for years. Now, don't lean your greasy head on the things!' she ordered in complete defiance of the purpose for which nature had evidently intended the chair-backs. 'Sit up straight!'

'Michty me, wumman, Ah think Ah'll go oot an' sit on the stairheid. It's been nothin' but dae this an' don't dae that since Ah came hame the nicht. An' a' fur the sake o' Jim M'Cotton's wife that's got as much sense in 'er heid as a flea!'

Just then Maisie came into the room to find her mother engaged in placing a heap of parcels on the settee. Asked for an explanation, Sarah said they were Christmas presents intended for exhibition to Mrs. M'Cotton.

'But surely we didn't get all those this year!' exclaimed Maisie.

'I know,' Sarah admitted, 'but I'm not going to let that woman M'Cotton do me in the eye. It's a shame, so it is, her getting a fur coat before me. You know quite well,' she turned to her husband, 'you've been promising me one for years, Willie!'

'But whit's the use o' buyin' mair deid beasts' skins when there's thae braw sheepskin rugs in the press there?'

'I say,' said Maisie, sniffing ostentatiously and without requiring any answer, 'what's the vile stink in here?'

'Och, it'll be this cigar,' answered Willie, taking another puff. 'Peter said he got them aff a man that worked on a boat,

but Ah'm thinkin' it's been a dredger this yin came affa. Ach !'
He made to fling the cigar into the fire, saying that he would be
better with his old clay pipe.

'I'll clay-pipe-you !' cried Sarah, preventing him from doing
what he wished. 'The very idea ! You'll just keep on smoking
that cigar till Mrs. M'Cotton comes.'

'Help ma boab, Serah, this isnae a cigar, it's—' he searched
for the metaphor—'it's somethin' that yince ran aboot on fower
legs but mortification has set in.'

The sound of the outside door opening made Sarah say,
'Wheesh ! There's Peter home now ! Try not to hurt his feelings about the cigars, Willie.'

As Peter opened the sitting-room door Willie murmured
a plea to be left alone to enjoy himself in peace. He added a
postscript about the dubious quality of the enjoyment that lay
ahead of him as per programme, but fortunately the finer points
of his remarks were missed by Sarah, who was busy answering
Peter's questions about the welfare of his small nephew.

'What's up that we're sitting here in state ?' asked the lad
at length.

'We're sittin' here,' replied his father with great deliberation
and with malice aforethought, 'waitin' fur Mrs. M'Cotton tae
come up an' let us see 'er new fur coat. Yer mother's tongue's
fair hingin' oot wi' excitement.'

'It is not !' retorted Sarah. 'If you'd had any decency in
you, you'd have seen to it that it was me who was showing off
the coat to Mrs. M'Cotton.'

'Ay-ay, Serah. Ye're a fine wee lass ! It's a peety ye drink !'

'D'you know, Dad,' commented Maisie, 'some day somebody will believe you when you say that to Mother in public.'

Sarah was about to concur with the complaint that she herself had been pointing that out for years when Peter got in with :
'I've got another present for the wee chap. What about getting
him up out of bed ? He could lie a wee while longer in the
morning, Mother.'

The wheedling tone was hard to resist, but Sarah's protests
were cut short by the sound of the door-bell ringing. As Peter

rushed to open the door his mother called after him, 'That'll be
Mrs. M'Cotton, Peter. Now mind—not a word to her about
wee Ian being here.'

In a few moments Mrs. M'Cotton's affected voice reached
them, and Sarah, looking round to see that the stage was fully
set, urged Willie to put on his slippers again. He was still forcing
his feet obediently into the refinement of tight black kid when
Peter opened the sitting-room door and announced :

'Here's Mrs. M'Cotton, Mother.'

'Oh, come in, Mrs. M'Cotton,' said Sarah. 'This *is* a
surprise ! Come over here beside the fire. You're just in time
to see all our Christmas presents.'

Mrs. M'Cotton, preening herself in the splendour of her own
present, replied, 'Oh, Eh'm afraid Eh haven't tehm to wait.
No, Eh'll not go too near the fehr. It'll be too warm for me with
meh fir coat.'

'Ach,' said Willie affably, 'take aff yer coat. Fling it ower
the back o' thon chair.'

The suggestion merely infuriated the owner of the fur coat.
'Fling it, did you say !' she snapped. 'Eh like thet ! Meh
new fir coat !' Turning to Sarah, she purred, 'How do you
like it, Mrs. McFlehnnel ?'

'It's quite nice,' said Sarah dispassionately. 'Won't you take
it off and Peter'll hang it on the hallstand ?'

But that suggestion pleased her no better than the previous
one. 'The hallstand !' she exclaimed. 'Eh'm beginning to feel
sorry Eh went to the trouble of coming up to let you see it.
Eh don't think you know a really good fir when you see one.'
She tried another direction. 'Maisie—what do *you* think of
it ?'

'M'n.' Maisie sounded dubious. 'Is it one of the new
synthetic furs ?'

'Of course it is ! Jim would never get me anything but the
best of everything. It's poneyskin.'

Exchanging a wink with her brother, Maisie merely said,
'Oh, yes ?'

Sarah got one in then. 'Is it not just a wee-thing on the

youthful side for you, Mrs. M'Cotton? After all, you're a grandmother. What do you say, Maisie?'

'Maybe,' Maisie rallied to her mother's support. 'For myself, I'm partial to musquash, but of course it's an awful price just now.'

'Well, Jim wanted me to get a musquash, but there just wasn't a decent one to be had. What about trehing it on, Mrs. McFlehnnel?'

'Oh no. Don't bother.'

'Come on,' coaxed Mrs. M'Cotton, sliding out of her Christmas present, 'you'll feel really well-dressed for once in your life.'

Before Sarah had time to express her feelings following the jibe, Willie got in with, 'Go on, Serah. Try the thing on. An' maybe Mrs. M'Cotton'll gi'e ye the pattren fur thae sheepskin rugs.'

'Willie!' Some of Sarah's fury with her visitor was finding expression in her vehement attack on her husband. 'If you say sheepskin rugs again, I'll—I'll . . .'

At that Peter wanted to know what all this was about sheepskin rugs, and his father was eager to oblige with the information, but his speech was strangled at birth by Sarah letting out a warning howl. Maisie stepped into the breach by saying, 'You must see our collection of presents, Mrs. M'Cotton.'

'Yes,' said Sarah, 'see—put your coat over the back of the settee and you'll feel the benefit of it when you go out.'

'Listen!' said Peter suddenly. 'I thought I heard something just now.'

'Yes,' said Mrs. M'Cotton. 'It sounded like a child crehing!'

Glaring her annoyance at Peter, Sarah said it must have been a cat. She hurried forward to exhibit the chair-backs Maisie had presented as a Christmas present. Not paying any attention to them, Mrs. M'Cotton laid her coat lovingly on the back of the settee after the manner of a window-dresser, saying, 'You're not as interested in meh fir coat as Eh thought you would be—but maybe you're a bit jealous. Jim said you would be!'

'What!' exclaimed Sarah with a grand show of indifference. 'Me jealous? Never in your life! I've got no great notion for a fur coat. I always think folk are overdressed in them, and see how bedraggled they look after a shower of rain.'

This statement was too much for Willie. In utter amazement he blurted out, 'But here, Serah, ye're jist new-done——'

Before he could complete his revelation, Sarah ordered him to put some coal on the fire, but more discomfiture awaited her, for at that moment Peter insisted, 'Mother, I'm positive that's the wee chap crying!'

Naturally Mrs. M'Cotton wanted to know what wee chap was referred to.

'Oh, ehm . . .' Sarah racked her brains. 'It's—ehm—the folk through the wall have a wee boy of six that cries a lot.'

'But Mother——' began Peter who had obviously forgotten his instructions.

'Hand over that square box, Maisie,' Sarah said hastily, 'till I let Mrs. M'Cotton see the new tablecloth I got from Mrs. McLeather.'

Mrs. M'Cotton, realizing that her mission had been in vain, lifted her coat which she had been stroking all the time and began putting it on, saying, 'Oh, Ehm afraid you'll have to excuse me. Eh simply haven't the tehm to spare. . . .'

Into the middle of her speech came the unmistakable wail of a sleepy, frightened child. The cry was so insistent that Peter got up and left the room saying he couldn't bear it any longer.

'Dear me, Peter seems *very* excited about something,' observed the visitor, struggling ostentatiously to find the armhole of her coat. She added, 'Maisie—would you like to help me on with meh coat? Not but what it slides on marvellously. It's gorgeous lehning, isn't it!'

Without giving Maisie time to reply, Willie remarked that Peter was fair set on the wee chap, so once more Sarah had to change the subject.

'Willie,' she said, 'are you sure you're not finding it too hot in here?'

'No' me,' said he affably; then in increasing geniality he

160

turned to Mrs. M'Cotton and inquired how her man was behaving himself.

'He's been asked for to speak at the Birns Club Dinner,' was the reply, given so unctuously that no doubt was harboured about the goodness of Mr. M'Cotton's behaviour.

'Look, Mrs. M'Cotton,' put in Sarah, 'what do you think of this lovely set of table mats?'

Mrs. M'Cotton looked with half an eye at the exhibit. 'Oh, thet remehnds me of the marvellous set our Jean made for me. Simply *gorgeous*, they are. Much finer than these!'

Sarah was spared the necessity of searching for a suitable retort; the door opened and Peter appeared with Ian in his arms. 'He says he wants to see his grannie!' he announced.

For a moment even Sarah was speechless; then she snapped, 'Peter! What did I tell you!'

As for Mrs. M'Cotton, she gaped at her grandchild, then managed to blurt out, 'Ian! What are *you* doing here! Eh thought you were safely tucked up in your own wee bed in Edinburgh. Come on and give your Grannie M'Cotton a kiss.'

Ian hid his face behind his uncle's head. 'No!' he declared flatly.

'Now, what kehnd of way is thet to speak to your grannie?' said Mrs. M'Cotton with an accusing look at her co-grandmother. She tried wheedling. 'Come on and Grannie will let you feel her lovely fir coat.'

'No.'

'Eh'd like to know why Eh wasn't told he was coming to Glasgow.' The accusing look was finding vocal expression.

'Oh, it was just a wee surprise visit for Christmas,' said Sarah.

'But it can't be good for the child to be living up a close! Eh suppose he'll have to sleep with his Uncle Peter. In any case, his father's people have more right to him than his mother's.'

Even Willie was aware of the imminence of a family squabble; he tried to avert it by making funny faces which Ian refused to look at, and which were inadvertently observed by Mrs. M'Cotton in the mirror above the mantelpiece, and which were interpreted as a further insult to her person. Peter then tried to create a diversion :

'Here, son, come on over here till you see what I've got for you.' He put the child down on the floor.'

'If it's another aeroplane, I don't want to see it,' announced Ian.

'No, it's a train, with signals and cabins and bridges.'

Soon the floor was strewn with the contraption, while the two grandmothers and the aunt were pushed aside to allow the grandfather, uncle and child to explore the possibilities of the toy. Willie, in his enthusiasm, bumped against Mrs. M'Cotton unwittingly.

'Don't shove meh fir coat like thet, Willie McFlehnnel !' snapped the coat's owner with rising irritation and huffiness.

But all Willie answered was, 'Ach, don't fuss. Peter—lift thon rug.'

Sarah, seeing that Mrs. M'Cotton was making no move towards the outside door, whispered to Maisie to make a cup of tea ; she added, 'I'll show Mrs. M'Cotton the presents while you're away.'

'Oh, don't trouble,' said Mrs. M'Cotton. 'Eh'm really just going. . . .'

'Look out, Dad !' shouted Peter, with the same boyish enthusiasm for a toy as his father. 'You nearly broke the lamp with that rail.'

Sarah watched her husband just miss crashing a china ornament. 'Oh, Willie, be your age !' she pleaded. 'You're far too old to be playing with engines.'

'Away an' bile yer can ! Heh, Mrs. M'Cotton—see's ower thon coupler that's lyin' at yer feet.'

For a moment it looked as though the lady were about to announce once again the urgency of her departure, but she stooped and picked up the required article and actually asked where she should place it. Willie directed her, and in a moment she was on her knees placing signal cabins, bridges, signals here and there on the line that by now occupied most of the sitting-room floor. Even Sarah got smitten with the fever, for she too wanted to know where she could put a tiny truck laden with milk-cans. Maisie left the room reluctantly. It was, she reflected surely the spirit of Christmas that was permeating the room, for otherwise she would have found it hard to believe possible that her parents and Mrs. M'Cotton would be on their knees together.

'Does this milk bar go on the station platform?' asked Mrs. M'Cotton.

'Ay!' replied Willie, who had constituted himself Traffic Organizer. 'An' thon bridge—pit it ower thonder aside Serah.'

'Would it not be better to put it over beside Peter?' asked Sarah, 'and then you could lead the roadway over it.' She demonstrated her point, crawling about on her hands and knees. All the gadgets of the second-hand outfit were at length assembled, and it was deemed opportune for the winding up of the toy engine—a model of the *Flying Scotsman*. Willie, as Master of Ceremonies, did not imagine that anyone else would want to wind the engine but himself. He did so with great relish, and as he placed it on the rails and it chugged its way along, all present, feeling they had each had a hand in its creation, cheered. That is, all present except the one for whom the toy had been intended. Their cheering was brought to a sudden stop as Ian let out a mighty howl of rage.

'I want to play with my own engine!'

'Aw, poor wee man!' exclaimed Sarah. 'What a shame! Here, Willie! Get up off the floor. And you too, Peter. Bundle all that stuff into its box at once.'

'But I want to play!' demanded Ian, bursting into tears.

'Now look what you've done, Peter!' Sarah, getting to her feet, accused her son. 'You and your engine.'

'It's *my* engine!' stamped the child.

Mrs. M'Cotton tried to create a diversion on her own. 'Ian!' she pleaded, 'come over here beside me and tell me how you're getting on at school.'

'I'm not at school!' answered Ian from the safe distance of the other side of the room. 'I'm at holiday.'

'Willie!' Sarah's voice cut into Mrs. M'Cotton's lesson on prepositions, 'put down that engine!'

163

Ignoring the marital dispute that followed, Mrs. M'Cotton made another attempt at befriending her grandchild. She went over to him. 'If your Gran'pa M'Cotton had known you were here, Ian, he'd of came to see you too.'

'It's a peety but whit he'd had a fur coat tae show aff forbye,' muttered Willie, obediently replacing the engine in its box. Ian, seeing the toy disappear, let out another yell to the effect that he wanted to play with his engine.

'Haud yer wheesht, son,' advised his grandfather, 'yer Auntie Maisie'll be here in a meenit wi' the tea. Wid ye like a bit cake ?'

'The very idea !' exclaimed Sarah. 'Cake at this time of night at his age !'

'I want cake !' The engine forgotten, Ian stamped all over again with his side-tracked demands.

'Eh tell you what, Ian. If you come over here and talk to me, Eh'll see thet you get a wee bit of meh cake,' suggested Mrs. M'Cotton, glad of the opportunity to undermine her rival's authority. The child showed signs of coming in her direction. She went on, 'Eh think it's lovely to hear him speak with thet nice Edinburgh accent. The Glasgow accent is so dreadful !'

'Div you no' speak wi' a Glasgow accent yersel' ?' asked Willie innocently.

'What, me ! Of course not ! Now, Ian, what about reciting something to your grannie ?'

'Naw !' replied Ian.

'Ian !' gasped his maternal grandmother. 'That's not the way to speak !'

'It's the way Granpa speaks !'

With a sigh and a look of inexpressible disgust at her husband, Sarah suggested, 'What about saying yon nice piece about the daffodils ?'

'Ugh no ! That's a girl's piece.'

'Well, is there anything else you say ?' asked Mrs. M'Cotton.

'No. Oh yes—I can say " Wee Willie Winkie." ' All the child's sulkiness was gone—his face was eager and pleasant.

'Och naw !' put in Willie. 'No' the nicht, son.'

'You hold your tongue, Willie!' said Sarah. 'If he wants to say "Wee Willie Winkie" then let him say it. Come on, Ian.'

But Willie was oddly reluctant to allow the suggested item to go on the stage. 'Never mind, son,' pleaded he. 'Ye're gettin' too auld tae say that.'

Peter, however, not realizing the distress in his father's voice, proved a broken reed, for he slapped the child playfully and said, 'I've never heard you say "Wee Willie Winkie." Cough it up —there's a good wee chappie.'

'Naw don't, son!' Willie was more importunate than ever.

'Willie! Will you stop interfering!' snapped Sarah.

'A'right!' he replied resignedly. 'On yer ain heid be it!'

The child needed no encouragement. He started out slowly, daintily; then, getting embarrassed his solo was finally rendered *accelerando, crescendo con brio* :

> 'Wee Willie Winkie rins through the toon,
> Upstairs, doonstairs, in his nichtgoon,
> Scartin' at 'is oxter, clawin' at his heid,
> Wishin' a' the fleas an' bugs that crawled
> on him wis deid.'

'Stop! Stop!' cried one grandmother.

'Ehbsolutely disgusting!' cried the other.

'Well, ye asked fur it!' retorted Willie.

'Ian, where did you learn that?' demanded Sarah.

'Eh'm sure they never learned him a thing like thet in any school in Edinburgh,' opined Mrs. M'Cotton.

'And I'm sure he never learned it at home!' snapped Sarah.

'I did so!' put in Ian. 'Granpa teached me it.'

'Eh, ya wee clype—ye!' groaned the author.

'Oh, Willie, you didn't!' moaned Sarah in unbelief and discomfiture. 'Oh, I never was so ashamed in all my life. Ian —away you go back to your bed this minute!'

'But I've to get a bit cake! You promised me!'

'All right! Peter—away you go to the kitchen and get a bit for him, and then take him back to bed at once.'

As the lad disappeared Mrs. M'Cotton remarked that she wondered what her son, the child's father, would say if he knew he had been taught such vulgarity.

'Ach away !' said Willie. ' Ah'm sure 'is Granpa M'Cotton could learn 'im a lot waur nur that !'

'What d'you mean ?' demanded the absent Granpa's wife.

'Och, nothin'. Jist that Ah've heard yer man comin' away wi' some gey broad yins.'

'It's a lie ! My man's a gentleman !'

Her manner as well as her tone brought Sarah to her feet, blazing out, 'Here, you—don't talk to Willie like that !' and in turn her manner and tone offended the visitor so much that she exclaimed :

'Oh ! Eh've never been so insulted in all meh life ! Eh'm going away to send a wire to Dick to tell him it's time he had Ian back to Edinburgh. Getting his mind filled with such dirty poetry.'

'Heh-heh !' called Willie. 'Mind whit ye're sayin'——'

'I'll mind all right !' she retorted with a slight deterioration in the veneer of her speech. 'I always said our Dick was far too good for your Polly.'

'Too good for our Polly !' Sarah's speech, too, was suffering under the strain. 'Get away wi' ye. Dick was nothing but a wee naethin' when Polly met 'im. She's *made* 'im.'

'A wee naethin' ! Our Dick ! Oh ! Oh ! If I wasnae wearin' ma fur coat, Ah—Ah'd bash ye !' declared the visitor, having gained complete freedom from the inhibitions of her class consciousness. 'Where's Ian ? I'm takin' 'im away wi' me.'

'Ian's away to bed !' said Peter from the door, and with a look of amused contempt on his face which Mrs. M'Cotton guessed was aimed at herself. In a fever of indignation she took her departure, colliding *en route* with Maisie, who was trundling the tea trolley towards the sitting-room. There was a splash of milk, a rattle of crockery, and a cascade of jammy tarts, one of which saluted the new fur coat in the by-going ; it was the only farewell salutation offered to the woman, for her host and hostess seemed rooted to the spot with surprise.

'What high wind's blowing her?' demanded Maisie, gaping after the slamming door. There was no reply, and the girl looked blankly from her father to her mother. She had a shrewd suspicion that the latter was on the verge of tears.

'It's all your father's fault!' said Sarah at length. The tears, never very far away from her eyes, welled up.

'Oh, don't cry, Mother!' said Peter. 'See, I'll pour you out a cup of tea. You'll feel better.'

'But what happened?' insisted Maisie. She turned accusingly to her father. 'Dad! You've said or done something to hurt Mother's feelings.'

'Me? Ah never done nothin'.'

'You did so!' Sarah was now weeping with abandon. 'Teaching Ian that dirty poetry.'

'Oh, Mother,' said Peter, pouring out the tea. 'It wasn't dirty—just a bit broad.'

'Now, don't *you* turn against me!' cried the affronted woman. 'Oh, I was never so humiliated.'

'Ach, screw aff the watter!' said Willie, not without some sense of guilt.

'You just *tried* to do it!' she went on. 'And if it had been anybody but that woman M'Cotton! And her with her new fur coat on, too.' She sobbed out the rest of her complaint. 'She despises me enough already, the bizzum.'

'Ach, cheer up! Ye never died a winter yet!'

'Oh, will you shut up!' Tears were giving way to a flyting temper.

Willie looked at his wife. His sense of guilt increased as he saw her tears and her vexation. 'Peter!' he ordered. 'See's thon parcel Ah asked ye tae bung in yer suitcase fur me.'

'Okay,' said Peter.

Sarah, in the welter of her grief, having missed her husband's remarks, now gaped at her son while he opened the door that concealed his bed and scrabbled about amongst the variety of tin trunks jostling one another in the space below. Before she could demand an explanation, he drew out a large parcel. Willie grabbed it, shoving it under Sarah's nose and saying:

'Here—look ! This is somethin' Ah wis keepin' fur ye till Hogmanay—oor weddin' anniversary, but maybe if ye get it the noo it'll make ye feel better. Ah—Ah'm real sorry fur—fur everythin'.'

'I don't want anything from you !' she said, drawing back from the parcel but eyeing it with great curiosity all the same.

'I'll open it !' said Maisie, darting forward. In a moment or two the brown paper was stripped off, revealing a froth of tissue paper underneath. When it in turn was removed a hairy object was seen. 'Boy ! Oh boy !' yelled Maisie in an ecstasy. 'Mother ! It's a fur coat ! Oh, Dad—where did you get it ?'

'A chap in the work has a sister in the trade,' said Willie, trying not to appear self-conscious. 'Ah spoke tae'm aboot a coupla month ago. Come on, Serah. Try it on.'

'What a beauty !' Maisie's enthusiasm was infectious. 'Look, Mother, it's dark musquash, the very best ! And see— it's the centre of the skins only that's been used.' She held it up with all the exhibitionism of a born saleswoman. 'Come on, Mother. Surely you can at least try it on !'

But Sarah had turned her back on the coat ; her face once more in her handkerchief, she stumbled blindly towards her husband, gulping, 'Oh Willie, what did you go and do that for ?' She found refuge in his shoulder, where she had her cry out, then, with one eye she peeped at the coat which Maisie was quite obviously contemplating trying on herself. 'Oh, it's too good for an old woman like me !'

Willie clapped her shoulder affectionately. 'Aw, heh, Serah, ye've been greetin' fur it fur years, an' noo that ye've got it ye're greetin' worse than ever !'

'Oh, Willie, I can't help it ! Here . . .' She reached up her mouth, 'I'll need to give you a wee cheeper.'

Willie accepted the kiss with some emotion—an emotion he strove to hide by slapping her shoulder more soundly than before and pushing her away with, 'Heh-heh, haud off ! Ye're spilin' ma shed. Come on—let's see ye wi' the coat on afore Maisie pinches it.'

Maisie held the coat open once more, and Sarah slipped her

arms into it. Peter, too, took a hand in the robing ceremony, saying that she would need to start talking Pan Loaf now like Mrs. M'Cotton. Sarah stroked the fur, preening herself like a bird and saying she felt real bien for the first time in her life. Together the family accompanied her to the wardrobe mirror in Maisie's bedroom, where she viewed herself from all angles, and made another attack on her husband's hairless coiffure. Maisie observed that it must have cost a bonnie penny.

' Ach, never mind that,' said Willie. He felt a hero, and was elated with the appreciation his family accorded him for having done the right thing for once in his life.

Sarah examined her reflection thoughtfully for a moment or two, then she said, ' I've just been thinking—it was—kind of nasty of me to say yon to Mrs. M'Cotton about Dick—you know, about him being a wee naethin'. I feel I—I ought to go right up the now and apologize.'

' The very dab ! ' said Willie. ' Whit aboot keepin' on yer fur coat ? '

' Of course,' she answered calmly. The tears that were still hovering on her lashes added a twinkle to her eyes as she added, ' That's why I'm going ! '

On VE-day the war in Europe duly ended, but not the war between Sarah McFlannel and Rubina M'Cotton, which was to go on and on and on.

PRINTED IN GREAT BRITAIN AT
THE PRESS OF THE PUBLISHERS